THE MIDNIGHT READING CLUB KILLS

A locked club ballot, a midnight bell, a body by the stacks

Copyright © 2025 by Ivy Grant

Cover designed by Azameti Michael

Published by Azameti Michael

All rights reserved. No part of this book may be reproduced, distributed, or transmitted in any form or by any means, electronic or mechanical, including photocopying, recording, or any information storage and retrieval system, without the prior written permission of the publisher, except in the case of brief quotations embodied in critical reviews and certain other non-commercial uses permitted by copyright law.

This is a work of fiction. Names, characters, places, and incidents are either the product of the author's imagination or used fictitiously. Any resemblance to actual persons, living or dead, or actual events is purely coincidental. For information about this title or to request permission for use, please contact:

greyama70@gmail.com

First Edition, 2025

BOOK FOUR

PEPPERMINT CAT BOOKSHOP MYSTERIES

TABLE OF CONTENTS

Chapter 1: Midnight Rules
Chapter 2: Lights Out
Chapter 3: Body Found
Chapter 4: Ballot Batch
Chapter 5: Timer Check
Chapter 6: Chair Scrape
Chapter 7: Cousin Angle
Chapter 8: Pod Tape
Chapter 9: Card in Jacket
Chapter 10: Ladder Foot
Chapter 11: Gran Remembers
Chapter 12: Rafi's Roster
Chapter 13: Phone Grid
Chapter 14: Alibi Crack
Chapter 15: Podcaster Panic
Chapter 16: New Member Past
Chapter 17: Vote Motive
Chapter 18: Full Scene
Chapter 19: Charges Split
Chapter 20: Club Reset
ABOUT THE AUTHOR

CHAPTER 1

Midnight Rules

We kept the circle tight. Eight chairs in a ring on the shop floor, spines to the stacks, knees to the rug. The Peppermint Cat logo sat small on the lockbox table like a stamp of intent. Phones stacked inside, screens down, sound off. Peppermint curled beside the lockbox as if he had invented security. He blinked at the room once and resumed his shift as a warm paperweight.

"Midnight Reading Club," I said. "House rules. No spoilers, no shouting, no secret recordings. If you need air, say so and take the alley door with a buddy. If you touch the breaker or the wall timer without asking me or Rafi, I will cut your card for a month."

Benji Hsu nodded like he had been waiting for rules. New member, early thirties, neat hands, a jacket that loved pockets. He had that watchful courtesy you see on librarians who left their old desks but not their habits.

Conrad Vale folded into a chair with the air of a man who wanted a throne. Landlord, numbers for blood, cousin to Erica. His shoes squeaked once on the wax we had laid yesterday in the travel aisle. He gave the circle a smile that did not land.

Erica Vale took the seat opposite him and stared at the clock with calm dislike. She wore a pale blue cardigan that drew the eye without trying. She had spent six months keeping tenants organized and another six telling Conrad no. She ran on purpose and coffee. I liked her.

Jenna Roarke claimed the chair near the travel shelf. Podcaster, wired for attention, good at making silence feel like a gap she could fill. Her tote showed a tripod leg peeking out like a stowaway. She had asked for permission earlier. I had said no to live recording, yes to a single room ambience clip if it kept her quiet. She smiled and promised taste. I do not buy promises with teeth marks.

Margo Ellsworth adjusted the hem of a blazer that wanted a panel stage. Moderator by vote, self-appointed shepherd of taste. She loved the phrase reading culture and said it the way people say religion when they want a tithe. She opened a manila folder and fanned out a neat stack of paper.

"New wrinkle," Margo said, voice level, smile snug. "We test a secret ballot tonight. Single question. Keep or remove a member from moderator duty next month." She looked at Erica without looking at Erica. "Ballots in the middle at half past eleven. We hold them until midnight for drama."

"Not here," I said. "No secret votes in my circle. If you want to remove a moderator you argue it in the light."

"The chamber does it," Margo said, as if the council's habits were scripture. "We borrow a page. It keeps peace."

"It keeps knives quiet," Erica said. She did not raise her voice. She did not need to.

Rafi lifted the lockbox lid and dropped a small key inside. "Phones down, people. If you need a photo for your feed, take it now. Then the box shuts."

Jenna flashed a grin and held up her phone for one last frame. The camera caught Peppermint's ear, the circle, the ballots on the table, and the brass of the wall clock at the back. She tapped out a caption with tonight and book emojis and slid her phone into the box with the rest. Conrad made a show of shutting his off. Benji had his powered down already. Erica set hers in without ceremony. Margo hesitated long enough to annoy me and then added hers with a noise that implied sacrifice.

I reached for the ballot stack. Standard letter cut. Crisp. A faint mark chased light across the top sheet. Not toner. Not dirt. A pattern hid in the fibers like a whisper. I tilted to the lamp.

Cat's-eye watermark. Two ovals with a slit, right where Gran had drawn it decades ago when she stamped her donation ream. Our shop used that ream for Blind Date Night last year. Gran's note on the ledger said we ran it dry by August.

"You printed these from our stock," I said. "How."

Margo's smile did not move. "It came from the club bin. You keep extras down here for events."

"There is no club bin," I said. "We never kept one. If I had leftovers from Gran's ream, I would not hide them under your logo."

Benji leaned in, not touching, eyes on the watermark. "It's pretty," he said. "Old-school."

"Rare," I said. "Also wrong for a secret ballot."

Margo slid the stack back to center, palms neat. "You are free to opt out, Liora. The club can still test process."

"On my floor we test with consent," I said. "No hidden structures. No stunts."

Rafi looked at the clock. "Twenty-eight minutes to midnight," he said. "I will check the breaker and the wall timer. We had a hiccup at five when I set the wax to dry."

"Do," I said. "And bring me the router page when you pass the office."

He nodded and moved to the back hallway. He walked like he always does when we run a night: calm and precise. He knows where every cord hides and which switch lies about its job.

I kept a hand on the ballot stack and slid the top sheet aside. Same watermark. Second sheet. Same. Third. Same. The bottom blank had a faint brown ring in the lower left, the exact shade our espresso machine gives a careless saucer. But our counter glass was spotless. I wiped it myself at ten. A coffee ring on a copier glass will print across every sheet if you do not clean it. The circle stood complete on the bottom blank with a nick you could line up later. I did not speak it now. The room did not need to taste my thoughts yet.

"Agenda," I said, pulling us back to purpose. "Short readings from this month's picks. One new title pitched for next month by each of you. Erica has the floor first."

Conrad shifted like a man who wanted to grab a mic. "I thought we were here to reset moderators," he said. "We agreed to air our issues with process."

"We can do both," I said. "We are not at council. We talk about books and the way rooms behave when power steps on people. Then we vote on next month's list. No secret anything."

Margo tapped the folder as if that could set the tone. "It helps to have a method," she said. "Clubs burn without structure."

"Structure without consent burns faster," Erica said. She opened a thin hardback and set a slip of paper on the first page she wanted. "I brought a short scene about a library that keeps its doors open in a storm. Not because it is noble. Because the storm exposes what the town already let rot."

Benji smiled at that line. Jenna started to lift her tote. I made the smallest no with my eyes. She sighed and let the tripod leg sink. Peppermint stretched one paw and tapped the lockbox for fun. The room breathed.

We read and talked. The shop's night rhythm wrapped us. Stacks kept their scent. The case lights along the rare nook glowed at half to keep dust honest. Rafi came back with a thumbs-up on the breaker. He had the router page pulled up on his phone. He set it near my chair.

"Dial's off," he said quietly, for my ear. "Physical timer wheel set to always on. I left it there. Router shows guest devices clean. No new joins since eleven. Names look like usuals."

"Thank you," I said.

He took his seat near the lockbox. Conrad tilted his head toward the back hallway as if he owned the ductwork. Jenna smoothed her skirt and sneaked a glance at the travel shelf. Benji wrote a quick note on a card with a tiny pencil and put it back in his pocket as if he paid rent to minimalism.

Erica read from her book. The passage was clean and sharp and made room for a person to think. It spoke about how storms do not create rot. They reveal it. She closed the book. Benji clapped once and then stopped himself in case clapping felt like a vote. We allowed a small smile to leak into the air.

Margo reached into her tote and pulled out a tablet sleeve. Black neoprene. Sleek. She unzipped it two inches, peeked at the corner within, and slid it back down the side of the bag like a magician putting away a coin. It was smooth, practiced, and out of place in a circle where phones slept in a box.

"Phone in the lockbox," I said.

"My phone is in the lockbox," Margo said, all innocence. "This is for notes if we need to reference minutes from last week."

"Minutes," Erica said, dry. "We read books. We do not pass ordinances."

"It helps the archive," Margo said. "Oral culture fades."

"So do staged nights," I said.

She did not rise to it. She patted the tote, settled the sleeve deeper, and folded the flap.

Jenna raised a finger as if a teacher could call on her. "Two notes," she said. "One. The reading was tight. Two. We do have to talk about moderator duty. Erica, you run clean. But the chamber likes a certain tone from our club and they leaned on Margo to keep a straight line with sponsors."

"We do not care about sponsors," Erica said. "We care about rent and books and a room where the person with the smallest voice gets to finish a sentence."

Conrad smiled with no humor. "The chamber cares about the same. They also care about rents paid on time and a public record that does not embarrass them."

"Public records do not bruise," Erica said. "Shoves do."

He flushed at that, small and fast. I filed it. Not a crime. A seam.

We rotated to pitches. Benji offered a novel about a small archive in a flood town. Jenna pitched a slick true-crime book with a brand I did not want in my shop. Erica pitched a slim essay collection about caretaking and public spaces. Margo pitched a hardcover that read like a donor gala. Conrad pitched a civic history that had investors on every second page. I kept notes the way I always do, in pencil, in a hand the court can read from three chairs away.

At eleven forty-five we took five minutes to stretch, refill water, and feed Peppermint a treat he did not deserve and knew he would still receive because he owns us. I checked the register, wrote a note for the morning shift about the coffee grinder, and returned to the circle with a fresh stack of blank cards for the next segment.

Margo eased the ballot pile toward the center again as if it had a will. "Half past," she said. "We test a quiet vote."

"Not without me," I said. "If you push this through, you do it in the open." I looked at the faces. "Raise your hand if you want to vote on removing a moderator tonight by secret ballot."

No hands. Jenna tried to read the room and chose to sip water. Benji looked at Erica and not at me and then shook his head for himself. Conrad tapped his shoe and said nothing. Margo kept her smile as if a different room had voted yes.

"Midnight bell in fifteen," Rafi said. He stood and went to the back to set the chime. The old wall clock had a habit of sticking. To keep the count honest we had wired a soft chime to a timer we normally used for closing checks. He tested it at five, then again at nine. A dry run would not hurt.

"Quick test," he called from the hall. "Lights dip on the chime for half a beat. Then back. Stay seated."

"No," I said, moving toward him. "Not without me there."

I walked the back hall with him. It held the breaker panel, the wall dial that controlled the old fluorescent line by the stockroom, the router cabinet, and the switch for the chime. We had replaced the wall timer wheel last year when the old one started to drift. The new one ticked like a polite beetle and rarely lied. I checked the wheel. Set to always on like he said. I checked the breaker labels. Clear. I checked the router. Guest network steady. No unknown devices. Our smart bulbs ran on a hub in the front bay, not on this dial. Everything matched the plan.

"On my mark," Rafi said. "Three, two, one."

The chime pinged soft and silver, a single note that would make a person smile if they trusted rooms. The overheads dipped for the count of a breath. In the circle, chairs shifted. The ballots whispered as they took one sigh of air.

When the light returned Margo wore a smile sized for a stage line. Not joy. Satisfaction. She glanced at her tote. Her hand smoothed the sleeve with the tablet hidden inside the bag.

"See," she said. "The room can handle a small drama."

"This room does not run on drama," I said, crossing back to my chair. "It runs on pages and proof."

Peppermint jumped down, inspected the base of the lockbox table, and sat on my foot as if he wanted to pin me to the floor. He does not break tension. He absorbs it.

We reset our seats. Rafi checked the chime again with his eyes, not his hands. The clock read eleven fifty. I made the circle look at the face the way a teacher makes a class look at a map. We would need our times later. We would always need our times.

Margo folded her hands as if in prayer. "At midnight," she said, "we mark a reset and turn a page."

"Not with a stack you cannot source," I said. "We vote on next month's list."

"After we test the ballot," she said.

"No."

I have learned you do not fill a room with no. You set it in the center like a brick and let the rest of the furniture arrange itself. It worked here. Jenna leaned back. Benji exhaled. Erica reached for her water. Conrad pulled his chair a hair closer to the circle as if a small adjustment could turn gravity.

The wall clock clicked. Forty seconds. Thirty. Twenty. Rafi looked at me and lifted his eyebrows. I nodded. He moved to the back hall again for the formal chime. A night like this needs a sound to mark it.

"You still plan a vote," Margo said. It was a statement, not a question. She kept her face soft.

"We plan a list," I said. "If you can keep your hands off my light switch."

She smiled. "Watch me."

The chime waited. The room waited with it. Peppermint twitched one ear. Jenna checked her tote with a toe. Benji rubbed the edge of his card with a thumbnail and put it away. Conrad measured the door with his eyes. Erica sat with her back straight and her jaw set like a line cut into stone.

Rafi called from the hall. "On the bell."

The clock ticked toward twelve. I set my keys by my knee. I felt the shop breathe. The old boards under the rug held, the case glass sang its invisible note, the rare nook kept its secrets as muted as only cloth and paper can keep them.

The light dipped again, a clean flicker for half a beat. Margo's smile sharpened. It looked like a point.

CHAPTER 2

Lights Out

The room took in a breath it did not deserve and held it for the clock.

Fifty-nine. The second hand climbed without a slip. I watched the tip cross the twelve. The bell pinged once in the back. Clean, soft, true.

Midnight.

Every light in the shop went black.

No slow fade. A cut. The kind that makes a person hear their own blood.

A chair leg scraped. Fast. Wrong direction. A breath at my right turned into a small scream, clipped hard at the end like a hand on a mouth. A shape caught another shape. Air moved. A heavy thud hit wood and then the shelf. The floor felt that weight and sent a dull answer up through the rug and into my feet. Another chair skidded with a sharp burst, the rubber foot hopping across wax and then settling with a small compliant sigh.

Time, I said, loud. Twelve zero zero, mark.

My hand went for my keys where I had set them at my knee. Fingers found the ring and not the table. I closed a fist on metal. Good.

Someone whispered no. Not a scream. A breath with a word

inside it.

I let the dark stay dark for one more count. It tells truths light refuses. I learned that in basements under bad bulbs and at counters where panic picks mistakes for you.

The smell of citrus wax rose from the floor near the travel shelf. Yesterday we laid it in that aisle and nowhere else. Fresh, bright, faintly chemical. In the dark it pushed at my nose like a note on a door. I cut that thought in half and let it sit. Sensations now. The story later, when paper can carry it.

A phone buzzed with a mean little sting on wood. Face down, muted, near my left foot. The light from the screen threw a keyhole glow across the edge of a chair leg. Green digits pulsed once under black glass. I did not touch it. I filed where it lived. Inches inside the arc of Margo's chair.

No one spoke for a full two counts. Peppermint gave a short offended chirp from somewhere near the lockbox table. He does not explain himself when the room fails to meet his standards.

Rafi, I said, at volume. Do not touch the breaker.

Copy, he said from the back, voice steady but closer than the hall. He had taken three steps toward us when the room snapped dark. He had stopped himself. I was thankful for that habit. The breaker could sit.

A small grating sound came from the direction of the travel shelf, metal on wood with a little bit of rubber that wanted to help. A ladder foot being dragged or kicked or set down wrong. I could not see the thing. I could hear its argument with the floor. It was a squeak more than a grind. The kind of sound you make when a weight wants down and the hand holding it wants it somewhere else and neither gets to vote.

Everyone hold your seats, I said. Keep hands visible. Count your breaths out loud. One.

One, Erica said, crisp, front right.

One, Benji said, a fraction delayed, front left.

One, Conrad said, behind Benji and to my left, rough from a held cough.

One, Jenna said, low and breathy from near the travel shelf.

One, Margo said, behind my right shoulder, sweet as a woman on stage and not as steady.

Two, I said. Keep going. Do not move your chairs.

Two, the circle replied, overlapping and human.

On three, the front bay glowed warm and weak, the house bulbs stepping back into the world like people who do not trust it. One strip along the bay first, then the second. The half lights in the rare nook woke last. The case glass picked up just enough glow to show us outlines. The wall clock stalled for a blink, then found itself and kept time.

Stop, I said. Nobody stand. Keep your hands on your knees. Rafi, stay where you are. Peppermint, try not to sue us.

Peppermint trilled and flicked a tail against the lockbox, as if to say my counsel will be in touch.

I took a breath and let my eyes catch up. The circle had changed without a ton of motion. One chair sat skewed, not out of the ring, but rotated three hands inward, as if someone had twisted it to make a space where a body could slip past. The track it left on the rug made a pale arc of pressure. The chair belonged to the seat Jenna had taken. The skew pointed not at the alley door. It pointed across the ring toward the lockbox table and the nearest end of the travel shelf.

Erica still had both hands on her knees. Her mouth held a line. No blood on her face. Good. Her pale blue cardigan had a pulled thread near the sleeve from a rough brush in the dark. She did not look down. Her jaw had that set that says keep the room still. I liked her more for it.

Conrad leaned forward, both palms open, a poor idea for a man who always wants his hands in other people's policies. He saw me see him and placed his hands on the tops of his thighs like a schoolboy told to stop. A smear of dull darker wax showed on his right shoe heel. It had the same citrus sheen I could smell. He had either stepped in the travel aisle after we closed or he had moved there now. I marked the heel in my mind and did not make him famous for it yet.

Benji sat back, eyes wide but not wild. The kind of wide that says you came here to leave a past behind and now the present wants to audition for your nightmares. He kept his space. His chair was still true.

Margo had both hands lifted an inch from her lap, as if she had been about to stand when the lights went and now had to pretend her body did not tell on her. The tote she had kept beside her chair had shifted a handspan toward the lockbox table. The tablet sleeve inside had turned so the zipper faced up like a grin. On the floor inside the arc of her chair leg, something flat and dark lay face down. The small light under it still leaked at the edge. A lock screen glow pulsed once and then again. Numbers lived on that light.

Do not move your feet, I said. Margo, leave that alone.

She tilted her head like a person being teased. Leave what, she said, bright. I did not drop anything.

A good lie does not blink. Hers did. It looked down and then up and did not land anywhere useful.

Jenna stood halfway, then pretended she had been stretching. She palmed something shiny from the shadow near her chair and let it fall into her tote in a single practiced move. The speed of it read ashamed, not proud. She kept her face calm for an audience that did not want calm from her.

Sit, I said. Everyone. Peppermint, hold the table if you need to look busy.

Peppermint put a paw on the edge of the lockbox and stared at Margo's bag with the focus of a small god ready to write a new chapter. Not a solver. A witness who likes to nap between depositions.

I stood with care, keeping my keys in my fist, and took two steps in a clock face toward the spot near Margo's chair. My boots made the floor talk in small ways. The citrus scent thickened near the travel shelf. The case light on the rare nook gave me a thin line to see by.

Phone, I said, pointing. Do not touch. Rafi, bring me the small evidence tray from the counter and the thin scale card. We will not make our whole life police theatre, but we will not step on our own toes either.

You have it, Rafi said from the back. He moved with purpose, not speed. He set the tray on the rug by my foot and slid the card to me. He did not glance at the breaker. He did glance at the router cabinet. Old habits made him check if a new device had popped up when it should not. I kept my face pointed at the floor. He did not need my eyes for that job.

I crouched. The phone lay face down, black glass marked with a shallow scuff at one corner. The edge lighting from the lock screen traced a thin green band around the glass and threw a ghost of digits onto the carpet. Not a call. A timer widget. A white wheel on a green field, the number fifty-nine shrinking toward a full circle and then flipping to zeros, then starting another count. The screen dimmed to sleep and then woke enough to keep the widget alive. The side button had a smear like lotion. The case had a small crack. I did not pick it up. I do not touch a thing until I speak its story twice.

Timer visible, I said. Face down. By Margo's chair. Green wheel active. It looks like a countdown at zero with an auto rerun. We will photograph before we move.

No one found that sentence fun.

Margo gave a soft laugh that sounded like a mistake. My phone is in the box, she said. That must belong to someone else.

We will test that claim, I said.

Jenna swallowed. She kept her gaze on the travel shelf and then forced it to my face. I did not reward her with a smile.

The shop settled another notch. The sound came back in layers. A fridge hum. A light flick in the case as a tube in the back needed a ballast. The near silence of seven people trying not to talk.

I pivoted my head toward the travel aisle without letting my feet leave the rug. A shape lay lengthwise along the endcap, half in shadow. I could see the bottom two rungs of the folding ladder tipped on their side. The rung caps showed one new scrape, pale, raw, and dirty with wax bloom. The opposite foot looked cleaner. I did not have the angle to see the whole length of the ladder. I did not have the angle to see if a body lay beyond it. The endcap blocked the view just enough to keep mercy out of reach. The clock kept time anyway.

No one moves, I said again, lower, ready to call out time for the record when we would need it. My voice had the tone it takes on when you run a private place that doubles as a public trust. It can make a landlord sit and a donor close a mouth. Not magic. Practice.

Rafi, lights on low only, I said. No breakers. No wall dial. Only the front bay slider. Then call Asa. He will ask the time. Tell him twelve zero two when the call connects. Tell him we held the room.

Yes, he said.

He slid to the front panel and took the slider for the bay bulbs up two fingers. The light pushed the dark back enough to give shape to our fear. Not reveal. Allow.

Jenna's chair sat skewed hard toward the shelf now that light had feelings again. I could see the path in the rug. A pale arc where weight had pressed and heat had lifted fibers. Fibers lie. Heat tells the truth. Someone had jerked that chair in the cut. She had to, to stand quick. She looked at the mark and then pasted on a neutral face that wanted to be helpful.

My phone was in my tote, she said. The first lie of the night that bored me.

Your phone is in the box, I said.

She palmed something again. Quicker now. Rafi saw it. He did not say a word. He does not perform. He remembers and brings it back when it pays.

Erica's hands had not moved. She demanded that of herself and delivered. She kept her chin level. She did not scan for a friend. She did not find an enemy. Her eyes held the travel shelf in their cup like a person holding a cup that contains a medicine she intends to swallow without ceremony.

Conrad wet his lips and looked at the back door with the kind of defensive hope a man gets when a plan wobbles. He had a rent plan on a clipboard in his car. He had that look.

Benji glanced to me and then to the phone on the floor. He did not ask to help. He knew the answer. He kept his jacket on and his face open.

Margo kept her smile a half inch wide. Her fingers pressed her knees. She liked to rehearse for rooms. She had not rehearsed this.

Time is twelve zero one, I said, for the record. We have a power cut that lasted one beat. We had a scream and a thud in the dark. We had a chair skidding. We have a ladder on its side at the travel shelf endcap. We have a phone face down by Margo's chair with a visible timer. We have all hands in sight. If you need water, wait for me to hand it to you.

Rafi put his phone on speaker and dialed Asa. The ring popped once and then he answered.

Tell me, Asa said.

Lights cut at midnight, I said. The bell hit true, then a blackout for one beat. Scream. Thud. Chair skids. Ladder on its side by travel shelf. One phone on the floor with a timer by Margo's chair. Room is seated. Time twelve zero two.

Hold, Asa said. I am on my way. Do not let anyone touch anything. If anyone pukes, point them to a bin and log it. Who is down.

Unknown from this angle, I said. Endcap blocks. I have a line on the ladder feet. One scrape shows fresh wax. Opposite foot clean. That matches our floor work yesterday.

Copy, he said. I will call Havel. Two minutes.

We ended.

I took the thin scale card and slid it near the phone without letting the edge touch glass. One photo first, then we would flip under the card and shoot the screen. Evidence needs its glamour shots like any diva. Only here the only fan is the clerk behind the glass at the Title Office.

Rafi handed me my shop phone so I could take the photo. We do not use our personal devices for this. The shop phone has a case that fits a scale card at the edge and a body that takes a beating when lawyers show up.

Photo one, I said. Phone face down by Margo's chair. Timer glow visible at the edge. Scale card north. Today's paper in frame.

I took it. I set the phone to the tray. I wrote one line on a tag. Then I slid the scale card under the black rectangle and flipped it like a pancake with a steady fingertip and the edge of the card as a spatula.

Screen on, I said. Timer widget at zero with a ring. Label shows Lights group in small text. Start time unknown. Repeat on. It sits unlocked behind a PIN skip. Whoever owns this device liked convenience more than security.

Margo inhaled through her teeth. She had the look of a woman who wants to tell a story about a neighbor's nephew. I did not give her a stage.

Do not speak, I said.

She did not.

The screen dimmed again and then woke on its own with a small haptic tick. It had a task to complete in a loop. That loop had lined up with the blackout at midnight. The wall dial in the back hall was set to always on. Rafi had checked it twice. The breaker sat where we left it. The smart bulbs we used in this bay could be grouped by an app. If a person had a device with that app open to a group called Lights or Peppermint Cat Guest, they could flip the entire group off and then on and keep the shop's wall dial honest and uninvolved. The green ring on the timer had the smug look that kind of control wears when it works. I do not hate electricity. I do not like being lied to by a widget in my own room.

Keep that screen awake, I said to Rafi. Photograph at fifteen second intervals for the next two minutes. We want a record of the loop.

He did. His hands do not shake on nights like this. He held the shop phone steady. He hit the shutter at the count. He looked at the face in front of him and not at the cast on the rug.

Jenna coughed small. She lifted her tote again and set it down as if that movement could erase the one she had made in the dark. Her chair stayed skewed. The rug mark would not redeem her. She knew it. She kept her profile arranged. A person can lie with a face if they have enough practice. We do not let faces testify, not without help.

Time twelve zero three, I said. Rafi, run the bay slider up another finger. Leave the rare nook low. I do not want heat on cloth until I know whose blood we carry.

He did. The travel shelf endcap took the light like a person receiving a coat. The ladder showed more of itself. The scratch on the left foot was raw and bright. A fleck of pale gray clung to the rubber pad. A peel pad from a floor kit lives on that face when new. When it falls off, the foot will scuff and grab and make a sound that bothers the part of your brain that evolved to hate sand in your shoes.

The opposite foot sat dark. No scuff. No wax halo.

The body beyond the ladder showed one shoe sole. Pale tread. Small. A blue sleeve. Erica's cardigan had left a fiber on her chair. The same blue lived at the end of that aisle on the floor. It could be a trick of color under this light. It could be the truth. I kept the shock inside my lungs where it would not clog my mouth.

Do not look, I said to the room. I am going to the aisle. Rafi, stand behind me, one step back. If I call a time, repeat it. Margo, if you touch the phone by your chair again I will put you out on the sidewalk and lock the door, and you will wait for Havel with your palms on your head.

She did not smile at that.

I stepped off the rug. The citrus pulled at me again. The ladder smelled like a spoiled orange. The aisle held the stillness that rooms make when they do not yet know what they contain. I kept low. I hate the way a fall reshapes a person. I also respect the moment. Respect needs space, not melodrama.

At the endcap I saw Erica's face. The blow sat on the right temple. The skin had already begun to swell. There was a shallow triangle of shelf varnish on the edge where the ladder had clipped it. The blood sat honest, not theatrical. It had not pooled far yet. My stomach tightened with that small relief you cannot put on a form. I put my own throat back down into the correct place and called the time.

Time twelve zero four, I said. Body at travel shelf endcap, head wound right temple, ladder on side. No breathing visible from this angle. No noise. No movement.

Repeat, Rafi said, steady. Twelve zero four. Body at endcap. Head wound right temple. Ladder on side. No breathing seen.

I pulled the thin roll of repair twine from my pocket and strung it across the aisle from one shelf peg to the other. I hung a handwritten tag on it the way I always do when we repair a stack. Not for repair. For respect and chain. Do not cross, evidence grid in progress, Wren.

Do you need me, Benji said from the ring. His voice had the tremble of a man who would rather reshelve a thousand misfiled atlases than watch a human being stop.

No, I said. Sit.

He did.

Jenna made a noise, then clamped it. She wanted to come with her lens. She wanted sound. She wanted to help. She wanted to not be blamed. All true. None helpful.

Conrad began to say something about votes and process and then saw the twine and swallowed the list he wanted to recite.

Margo finally looked scared. Not guilty. Scared in the way people get when consequence, which used to live as a word on a poster, stands in the room and asks them to pronounce its name.

Rafi moved to the counter and took the old bell in his hand. He would sound it once for the paramedics when Asa told us they were a block away. The bell is not drama. It is signal. It tells strangers where to put their feet.

The timer phone pulsed again. The green ring spun and completed and then spun again. I wanted to step on it. I did not. I let it sing its little song while we wrote what it did to the room.

Havel will ask you what you did at the blackout, I said without turning. If you moved, say it now. If you stood, say it now. I will put it in my book and Asa will take it out of my mouth and put it in his.

I did not move, Erica said. Voice steady. The sound of a person who refuses to lie as a matter of policy.

I reached for my water, Benji said, honest even if it put him on the wrong side of a line. My hand stopped when the lights cut. My chair did not move.

I took a breath and stood, Conrad said. I did not leave my chair. I did not touch the back door. Not then.

I looked at my tote, Jenna said. I thought it would fall. I stood to catch it. The chair must have shifted. I sat back down.

I kept my hands on my knees, Margo said. This is a tragedy. We can process it with care and then return to structure.

Peppermint made a small annoyed sound. He does not take language about structure from people who would use it to sell a party.

Asa called back. En route, he said. Havel with me. Rank the room from least likely to fall over to most likely. Keep the most likely seated furthest from the aisle.

Least likely, Erica, I said. Benji next. Then Conrad. Then Rafi. Then me. Most likely Jenna, then Margo.

I heard the flick of his pen in my ear. Good, he said. Do not move them now. We will organize elbows when we have eyes on the path. Did the blackout align with the timer you saw.

Yes, I said. Screen shows a group label. It looks like a smart bulb set. The wall dial was off earlier. We have not touched it.

Copy, he said. Bag the phone if you can keep the screen alive long enough for a photo. If not, get the timer screen at every change for the next minute. We will match that to the router log and your chime.

We are on it, I said.

He hung up. He knows when I do not need comfort and when people in my room need my sentences to be short. Tonight my sentences did not need ribbon on them.

Ears, I said to the circle. Listen to the shelves. If you hear a drip, call it. If you hear the soft high whistle people make after a head hits something they did not expect, call it. If you hear your own fear trying to tell you a heroic move would make you feel better, tell it to sit down.

Jenna rubbed her fingers together and said nothing.

Margo stared at the timer until it went black again. She twitched when it lit. The green ring had a power on her that she had not planned when she slipped her tablet sleeve into her tote.

Rafi timed his shutter clicks with the wheel. He marked the seconds out loud so the file would sync. Twelve zero five fifteen. Twelve zero five thirty. Twelve zero five forty-five. Twelve zero six. He set the shop phone down and put his hands on the counter. He swore softly and cleanly, a simple word no court will ever fault you for.

The bell at the front door gave half a cough as the wind from the alley walked the street and made the glass think about its hinges. I wanted to throw the bolt. I did not. Amber light from the bay warmed the frame. Outside, an ambulance siren decided our block would be its next note. In the back, the router vertex blinked a stable green. No new joins. No friend in disguise. The app had already done its trick.

I looked at Erica. Her mouth quivered once, then stopped. She met my eyes and said a single clear sentence.

I did not fall.

I believe you, I said.

Margo finally said the two words that had been chewing the inside of her mouth since the dark.

My phone.

Not now, I said.

It is in the lockbox, she said. If that is a phone, it is not mine.

We will see, I said. You may have two.

Her face did not like that. She bit the inside of her cheek to keep it from telling us how much.

Jenna shifted. Her chair squeaked on the rug again. The skidding foot of the chair lined up with the pale arc it had already drawn. She looked at the endcap and then at her tote. No one cheered.

Benji kept his hands visible. He showed me a left palm with a faint glue scar on the heel that told me he had worked with cover cloth in his life, not only with catalogues. He looked like a man who would not enjoy the next hour and would not leave simply because enjoyment had left.

Conrad leaned his elbows on his thighs and stared at the back door. He wanted to be outside where the air could hum at him without judging. He stayed seated because he had heard what I would do to him if he moved. I did not mind being predictable.

Peppermint lay down in a loaf with his front paws tucked, tail around his hip, eyes half shut, case file of a cat who considered this whole episode a failure of management.

The ambulance lights threw a wash across the window. Red across spines. Blue across jackets. My shelves looked like they were dressed for a parade they did not want.

Rafi stood with the bell ready. He tilted his head toward the travel shelf and then toward me as if to ask permission for his own heart to act. I shook my head once. Not yet.

Time twelve zero seven, I said. Power restored. Room held. Skewed chair remains. Phone at Margo's chair shows timer cycle. Ladder on side by travel shelf. Body on floor beyond, out of direct sight of circle. Head wound visible. No movement yet. Asa and Havel en route.

Jenna palmed her phone again, one last small slide like a gambler pocketing a chip under a sleeve. I saw it. Rafi saw it. The light glinted off the corner. She placed it under a folded scarf in the tote. The scarf was not thick enough to hide her guilt.

I made myself speak the last line for the page. It had the shape the city always takes when it wants to test you.

One chair sits skewed. We waited.

CHAPTER 3

Body Found

I took two steps down the travel aisle and let the floor tell me what it knew. Citrus rode the air from yesterday's wax. Fresh. Wrong here.

Erica lay lengthwise at the endcap, right temple to the floor, shoulders square, legs bent at an angle that spoke of a fall, not a laydown. No reach pose. No defense. Her pale blue cardigan had bunched under one shoulder and showed a pulled thread, the same snag I saw on her chair. Her cheek pressed the rug. Blood had tracked a short fan under the temple, honest and dark, not much yet. Her chest did not move under the knit. Her mouth had a pinch from teeth catching a lip on impact.

The folding ladder lay on its side between the last chair in the circle and the endcap. Two rungs visible, caps bruised. I crouched and looked at the feet. The left rubber pad carried a new gray scrape with a chalk bloom to it. I touched nose to air and got citrus and the faint powder note you get when wax meets friction before it cures. The opposite pad was clean. No haze. No transfer. A swing takes one foot light and drops the other hot.

Time twelve zero eight, I said, for the room and the camera. Ladder on side. Fresh gray scuff on one foot with citrus wax odor. Opposite foot clean. Victim unresponsive. Head wound right temple.

Rafi stood at the aisle mouth, one step back like we practice. He repeated the time and the lines and did not let his eyes betray him.

I pulled repair twine from my pocket, ran it shelf to shelf at hip height, and tied a square knot I could undo under a thumb if the paramedics needed a clean path. I hung a tag from the string. Do not cross. Evidence grid. Wren. Date. Time. I took a fast photo with the shop phone and set the scale card at the base of the ladder foot with the scuff. One shot of the foot and pad. One shot of the opposite pad. I said what the shot held before I hit the shutter. This is how you write a night so it survives daylight.

The shop bell coughed as the wind shoved weak through the door seam. Peppermint climbed the shelves like a small auditor who had paid the dues. He reached the top of the travel section and sat with his paws tucked, his tail wrapping a tidy half circle. He blinked at the ladder and then at me. Texture, not help. Good. He kept his place.

Rafi lifted the bell on the counter and gave it a single strike when the ambulance lights swept the glass. Signal, not drama. I heard Asa in that sound. He would be in the door in seconds with Havel at his shoulder. I let myself want that for a count, then got back to work.

Erica's pulse, I said, and slid two fingers to the angle of her jaw while keeping my wrist off the blood. No beat under skin. No breath at the mouth. Jaw slack, teeth not clenched. I pulled my hand back and looked at my glove, then said it for the page.

No pulse. No respiration. Time twelve zero nine.

I scanned for the thing that turns a fall into a second crime. No extra objects under her. No glass. No hard corner that did not belong to shelf or endcap. The thud we heard came from weight, not a surprise weapon. The ladder had done a piece of the job by accident or intent. Our reenactment later would tell me which.

Rafi handed me clean gauze in case the paramedic wanted first pressure for optics. I held it ready and did not touch the wound. We do not play at care when care cannot arrive in time. We hold the line and keep the chain.

Voices at the door. Asa first. "Nobody stand," he said as he entered, voice like a ruler laid on a page. "Havel behind me."

Havel went past him to the aisle. He did not step over the twine. He looked under it and then at me. We traded the quick nod two people trade when they have learned to meet grief with systems.

Time twelve ten, I said. Lights at fifty percent. Ladder on side, scuff described. Opposite foot clean. Victim no pulse.

Havel's eyes touched the ladder feet, then the scuff, then the floor. He breathed in, caught the citrus, and logged it without a word. Asa moved to the circle and set his case on the lockbox table. He did not even glance at Margo's tote. He would take that parade later.

"Phones stayed in the box," I said to him.

"Except the one with a wheel on the floor," he said, still mild.

"Timer app cycling a smart bulb group," I said. "Rafi has a photo series of the widget every fifteen seconds."

"Good," he said. He put on gloves and looked at the skewed chair, the arc in the rug, and the lockbox. He did not speak the conclusions he could pull. He made a slow ring around the circle with his eyes, then fixed on Jenna's tote for a long beat. He filed it for later like a man who likes dessert but knows better than to ruin his own appetite.

EMTs entered. Havel pulled the twine aside and lifted it over their shoulders, then let it fall back to the knot when they had passed. They worked with the quiet you get from people who do this often and resent being watched. They checked the jaw, the airway, the pulse, the pupil. One spoke for the record. No pulse. Pupils blown. Time twelve eleven. They gave me a look that asked me to turn down the shop while they performed the most formal minute. I dimmed the bay two points. They stood and covered Erica's face with a light sheet because the city has rules about who gets to see which lines when.

Jenna made a breathy sound. Asa looked at her and she shut it.

"Secure the aisle," Havel said to me, as if I had not already done it. Rituals matter. I tightened one knot and photographed the tag again. I marked the ladder feet a second time with the scale card. Rubber pad. Scuff. Citrus. Opposite pad clean. One close-up of the scrape to show grit in the gray bloom. We would match that to the bottle in back with the same chemistry and shade.

"Rafi," Asa said, not raising his voice. "Router admin."

Rafi slid to the back and pulled the page up. He had it almost ready from the first check. He read it aloud so Havel could hear. "Guest network shows no unknown joins. Device names on since eleven. One address labeled ME-TAB cached last seen last week. Not joined now. No fresh MAC since ten fifty-nine."

"Wheel phone," Asa said, pointing with his chin at the black glass on the floor. "Keep it awake. We will bag it under seal with the screen live if possible."

"On it," Rafi said.

Havel lifted his notebook. "Everyone," he said to the ring. "You will give a single sentence of where your hands were during the blackout. Liora repeats the time as each of you speaks. We will keep it to time and hands."

I stood where I was and let my voice carry. The room obeyed.

Erica's sentence sat in my throat but had nowhere left to go. I swallowed the fact of it and kept to the system.

"Benji," Havel said.

"Left hand on my knee," Benji said. "Right hand on my water. I did not lift it. Time twelve twelve."

"Conrad," Havel said.

"Both hands on my chair," Conrad said. "Feet on the rug. I did not stand. Time twelve twelve."

"Jenna."

"I stood one second to catch my tote," she said. "One foot moved my chair without meaning to. I sat down when Liora said time. Time twelve thirteen."

"Margo."

"Hands on my knees," she said. "I did not move. I said one word. No. Time twelve thirteen."

Asa wrote one word for each of them and then set the pen down as if he might stab someone with it if they made him write adjectives. He looked at me. I did my line.

"I called time," I said. "I reached for my keys, stood when the lights returned, and moved to the aisle. Time twelve thirteen."

Peppermint shifted his loaf to a sphinx, bright eyes on the ladder pad with the scuff. He blinked slow like it offended him. He had taste.

I held the paramedics' eyes and gave them space to finish the minute. One shook his head once and signaled Havel. He drew the thin sheet over the temple to free our view of the floor. Havel nodded. They stepped back without drama.

"Photograph the pad transfer," Havel said.

"Done," I said. "Odor noted."

The EMTs left with a promise of a coroner on call. I wrote the time they gave the formal line and logged it under initial assessment. No attempts at resuscitation. Blunt-force trauma suspected. Time twelve fourteen.

I looked at the foot of the ladder again. A tiny curl of pale gray clung to the lip of the rubber where the scuff changed texture. A peel pad corner. I did not touch it. I placed the scale card near it and shot it for the file. In back we had a partial pack with one pad missing from a purchase at 5:12 p.m. That shelf would close a loop later.

Havel pointed to the skewed chair. "Mark the arc," he said.

I did. Scale card at start of drag. Scale card at end near the lockbox table. One long shot showing the angle in relation to the travel shelf. I placed a blank card on the chair seat with the label

Jenna's seat, time twelve fifteen, chair rotation toward ballot box and travel shelf. Rafi took one with the shop phone too. Backup always pays.

Asa looked at the lockbox and then at the table near it. "Where did the phone sit," he said.

"By Margo's chair leg," I said. "Timer widget alive. Green wheel."

He crouched and took a long look at the screen without touching it. "Group label shows Lights," he said. "Not our wall dial. This is app control."

"Margo said her phone is in the box," I said.

He did not smile. "I heard her."

Margo kept her gaze on the floor. She wore the fixed expression of someone trying to hold a position in a river. It never works.

Peppermint stood and stepped along the shelf edge like a tightrope walker, then sat above the endcap and blinked at the ladder again. He looked like a bookplate without learning to be self-conscious about it. The ladder reflected a sliver of bay light back at him. He squinted. He had seen worse performances on this floor.

"Conrad," Havel said. "Shoes."

Conrad showed his soles like a boy at an airport. The right heel carried a small smear of dull gray with a trace of citrus when you bent toward it. I bent and did not comment. Havel did.

"You stepped in the travel aisle after hours," he said.

"I walked to the window," Conrad said, too fast. "After the club. I needed a call. The floor was wet then. I told your clerk not to worry, I would pay for damage to my shoes."

"You told my clerk nothing," Rafi said.

Conrad flushed and looked at the back door where the smart lock sat behind a steel frame that keeps out most lies. He would not win here. He knew it. He sank back one inch and bit the inside of his cheek the way his cousin had.

Asa turned the bay lights up two points and then down one to find the tone that gave us detail without glare. He does that like he breathes. He looked at my twine and nodded once. He looked at the endcap and the shelf varnish nick and nodded again. He stepped to the lockbox, checked the lid, checked the key inside, and closed it.

We held the room. We did not let story write itself without asking permission first.

The coroner arrived with a gurney and a bag that held the tools nobody wants to see in a bookshop. We let them in. We stepped back. We recorded what they needed and what they did not.

While they worked, Asa touched my sleeve and angled his head at the counter where the router admin page sat. "Peppermint Cat Guest," he said softly. "We will pull the DHCP leases later. I want the cached device names and the last time ME-TAB visited our network. If that tablet belongs to Margo, this room will prove it without arguing."

"Rafi saw the name," I said. "He knows where to pull a printout without waking the dragon."

"Good," Asa said.

Havel stood in the mouth of the aisle and rolled his pen under two fingers like a metronome. He asked me to state it again for the file and for the city and for the future memory of this room.

Time twelve seventeen, I said. Body fixed at endcap. Ladder on side. Left foot shows fresh gray scuff with citrus wax odor. Right foot clean. Aisle sealed with twine and tag. Phones in lockbox except one face down by Margo's chair with a timer group labeled Lights. Circle seated. One chair skewed toward the ballot box and shelf. Asa and Havel present.

I said it standing in my shop under light that knew how to treat paper. The words sat where they were put. That is how we live. That is how we make nights like this survive their own noise.

CHAPTER 4

Ballot Batch

We moved the paper to the counter because paper tells the truth there. Good light. Flat surface. Camera sightline. Till closed.

"Asa," I said, "we log the ballots now or after your first canvas."

"Now," he said. "We do not let a stack breed myths."

Rafi brought the lockbox key, a clean tray, sleeves, and the scale card. Peppermint hopped to the far end of the counter, sat by the receipt printer, and narrowed his eyes at the stack like an auditor with fur. Texture, not help. Fine.

I set the ballots in two piles. Left for filled, right for blank. The top three showed ink. The next carried a faint pencil hash that wanted to be a vote but would not survive adults. After that, a run of blanks. All were cut from the same stock. Same tooth. Same tone. Same faint pattern in the sheet when I took it to the light.

Cat's-eye watermark. Two ovals with a slit, placed exactly where Gran set it when she had the ream made for our blind date covers years back. It sits proud in a raking light and hides in flat light. On these ballots it looked pleased with itself.

"Watermark on every sheet," I said. "Not a copy onto cheap paper. Someone fed marked stock into a printer or copier."

Havel stood on the customer side of the counter, notebook low, eyes engaged. "Who controls that mark," he said.

"Gran," I said. "One donation ream. We ran it through last summer. I logged the end in the supply ledger."

Rafi had his phone already out with the ledger photo from August. He slid it over. The entry read Cat's-eye ream finished, blind date night, August 14. One tiny star beside it in Gran's hand. She marks endings the way some people mark births.

Margo stayed in a chair across the way with her hands folded as if a room would reward good posture. Jenna hovered at the edge, too eager to see without admitting it. Benji sat where I had told him to sit and looked like he wished the day had chosen a simpler story. Conrad stood by the community board with his jaw clenched and his shoe heel still wearing a smear of yesterday's work.

I held the top filled ballot to the light. The mark showed. The ink read thick ballpoint. The line of the printed header sat crisp, not inkjet fuzzy. I held a blank to the light. Same mark. The bottom blank showed something else.

"Set this one aside," I said, and laid the bottom blank near the scale card.

A ring sat faint and gray in the lower left quadrant. Not liquid on our paper. Toner or drum dust printed as a shape, not a stain. A coffee cup circle, ghosted and consistent. The exact nick in the circle repeated where a chip would sit on a mug rim. I laid three filled ballots beside it and found the same faint ghost in the same place at the same size. You would not see it unless you went looking. We were looking.

"Glass ring," I said. "Some copier has a cup ring on the platen. It prints into the corner of every copy unless you wipe it."

Rafi took a photo. "Our glass is clean," he said. "I wiped it before we closed, because I get to live here."

"We test anyway," Asa said. "Make a control."

Rafi pulled a blank from our plain stack, not the ballot stack, laid a sheet on our copier, hit copy, and brought the result. White corner. No ghost ring. He did it again with a second sheet and a bit of dust. Same result. Clean.

"The ring is not ours," I said. "It rides on another platen. Same position and nick on every ballot."

Havel wrote a line and did not look surprised. "Who has a copier that prints your group's headers," he said.

"The council chamber," Conrad said, too fast. "Everyone uses it, so the city lets clubs print a limited stack if our logo lives at the top. It is cheaper than a print shop."

Margo lifted a hand and made a face like a priest. "We have a community resource," she said. "We might as well use it."

"The chamber copier keeps a coffee ring on the glass," I said. "That is your community resource."

Benji's smile flickered and died. "Of course it does," he said.

Asa nodded to the stack. "Chain it," he said.

I put on fresh gloves, counted each sheet out loud into the filled pile, and numbered the backs in pencil at the lower right. One through eight filled or attempted. The rest untouched. I took a photo of the count with today's paper and the clock. Rafi bagged the filled pile in a sleeve, then bagged the blanks aside from the bottom three for later tests. I slipped the bottom blank with the ghost ring into its own sleeve and wrote the line. Faint platen ring image, lower left, repeated on filled ballots. Not our copier. Time twelve twenty-five. I signed across the tape and slid it to Asa. He signed under my line and set it near his case.

Havel looked at the filled stack. "Wording," he said. "Read it."

I read the printed header. Midnight Reading Club Procedural Vote, Moderator. Keep or Remove. Then a line about civility. Then a checkbox list. Keep, Remove. No name printed, but a blank for it. The font read house standard for the chamber memo template, down to the dull serif nobody loves and everyone uses because a committee once chose it. That would pay later when we pulled Margo's print queue. For now, we kept to paper and what it consented to reveal.

"The bottom blank shows the ring," I said again, to set it in the room. "Which means the whole run came from the same platen with the same fault. The watermark means the user fed marked stock into that copier."

"Might be the library," Jenna said. "They have a machine too."

"Which we maintain ourselves," I said. "You spilled coffee there last spring and I cleaned the glass while you vaped in the alley. It does not carry a ghost ring in the corner."

"I do not vape," she said.

"You do," I said. "We are not in church."

Asa watched our faces and said nothing.

Rafi slid the lockbox key from the tray and palmed it. He did not have to be told. He popped the lid, showed Havel the sleeping phones, and kept one hand on the hinge.

"Let us match a serial," Asa said.

I nodded. "One ballot from the stack. We hold it to the light and find the mark. See the slit position, cat's-eye. Gran's placement sits two inches from the short edge on this cut."

Rafi handed me a blank. I held it up. The ovals winked in the downlight. The slit sat right of center on the lower half. I put it down. I took a filled one and saw the same mark in the same place. Every sheet, same.

"Margo," Asa said. "Source."

She smoothed her skirt. "Club bin," she said. "We keep leftover event supplies in a bin by the back of the case."

"There is no club bin," I said. "There is a shop bin. I keep labels, pens, tickets for story time, and string. No ballot stock. No donation reams."

She shrugged. "Then the bin moved."

"Bins do not move without a body," I said. "You did not ask my body."

She smiled like a person on a panel who thinks a laugh will carry the room. It did not.

I set the cat's-eye close to the camera lens. "Gran's ream ran out last summer. She circled the line in her ledger. I will call her now to put it in ink."

Asa nodded. "Short call. Put her to time."

I called. Gran answers when I ring, midnight or noon. She does not waste the first seconds on greeting.

"Are you safe," she said.

"We are," I said. "We need your memory. Cat's-eye ream."

"Ran out the week of blind date night last summer," she said. "I wrote it in the book. Why."

"Ballots printed tonight carry that watermark," I said. "We are chaining them. I will bring you the ledger in the morning for a signature."

"I will be awake then too," she said. "Do not let that moderator girl tell you she found a secret stash."

"She already did," I said.

"Please," Gran said. "She calls order a decor theme. Good night."

She hung up. She never says goodbye. She assumes we meet again until we do not.

I turned the phone so Asa could see the call log and read the time with me for the page. Time twelve twenty-nine. Gran confirms the ream ended last summer. I wrote it on a card, signed, handed it to Asa. He tucked it under his pen as if it were a paperweight with a purpose.

Havel tapped the bottom blank sleeve with the back of his pen. "Where lives that ring," he said. "If not here."

"Chamber copier," Conrad said again, softer, as if volume changed facts.

"Name the room where it sits," Asa said.

"Copy alcove outside the council clerk's door," he said. "It is the public one. The building prints a lot of flyers. Somebody always parks a mug on the glass. It drives the clerk mad and she gives up."

"Who has after-hours access," Havel said.

"Anyone with a card," Conrad said. "Most people wait till morning. Some of us work late."

"Some of us bring a stack like this out the back door at ten," I said.

Margo kept the smile pasted on and let her eyes go glassy as if the night had done it to her. "You are making a stack into a story," she said.

"It already is one," I said.

Rafi slid a ballot from the filled sleeve and held it near the bottom blank. He lined the ghost rings. The nick in the ring matched. He rotated the page to test if a printer tray had been turned. The ring stayed married. He wrote a small centering note and then stepped aside so Havel could see without being told to.

"Photograph the overlap," Asa said.

I did. Scale card. Today's paper. Two sheets, nick aligned, ring ghost in frame. He signed the back of the photo label with me, then had me write the description on a card. We do all this boring work because drama lies and boredom points.

"Open the filled ones," he said next.

I counted the filled ballots back into the tray and walked through each with a gloved finger. Two check marks in Keep. Four in Remove. One blank with a line drawn local elections on the header in a rattle that read like someone trying to be funny. One half check in Remove, aborted. Names on the bottom lines differed by hand. One in a careful print that looked like a grandma who obeys forms. One in a tidy school hand that looked like people who teach others to hold a pencil. One in a slant that too many men use when they want to look important. Margo's had no name written. There was not a line for signatures anyway.

"Do not read us handwriting sermons," Havel said. He has a soft spot for methods that do not flirt with bias.

"I will not," I said. "I will read what the paper offers. Eight sheets were present. Some stayed blank. Enough ink for a stunt, not a meeting."

Asa wrote numbers and checked them. He compared the totals to the number of people in the room and frowned. "We had six at the circle, less Erica," he said. "Eight ballots marked for a test we did not consent to."

"Margo prints ahead," Jenna said, wanting to help and not sure it would save her. "You know, for outreach. She is a planner."

"Planner," I said. "Good word for a person with a sleeve full of hardware in a room where the rule says phones sleep."

She colored. She had the decency to look guilty and the instinct to hide it.

Rafi locked the box and kept the key in his palm where I could see it. The phones slept inside. The timer phone sat on the tray and pulsed its small green nothing. The ghost ring on the bottom blank sat in its sleeve. The watermark on each sheet waited to take us to Gran's garage when the sun arrived. Later. Not yet.

"Chain on the stack," Asa said.

"Cards on each bundle," I said. "On the filled sleeve, on the blank sleeve, on the bottom blank with ring, on the top filled one with the ghost. Each card reads where, when, who saw, who bagged. My hand and yours."

We wrote them. We signed. Peppermint watched us write and pretended to be bored.

Havel looked at Margo and spoke in that steady voice he uses when he offers a person their narrow path out of a hole. "Where did you get the stock," he said.

"The club bin," she said again, and let the lie sit still, as if repetition could buy it citizenship.

"There is no club bin," I said. "You are not at the chamber. You are on my floor."

"Then check your storage," she said. "Maybe your clerk put it there."

Rafi smiled as if a joke had run into him. "My name is on every bin in this shop," he said. "I can recite contents by memory and by tag. If cat's-eye sat anywhere but the board in Gran's garage, I would know it."

Asa let the silence answer Margo for us. He turned to me. "Photograph the counter scene," he said. "Stack, ghost ring, bagged sets, lockbox, time on the wall. Then we get back to the aisle."

I did. One wide shot. One of the stack with the cat's-eye in raking light. One of the ghost ring. One of the lockbox lid and the key in Rafi's palm. One of the time with hands at half past twelve. I spoke the time again for the camera, and for the room, and for this shop which puts order in paper before it lets fear have a word.

"Time twelve thirty-four," I said. "Ballot stack logged. Watermark on all sheets. Bottom blank carries a faint cup ring that repeats on the filled ballots. Our copier glass is clean. This ring lives somewhere else. Phones remain in the box. The timer phone sits in a tray."

Margo looked at the stack and tried again, as if practice could make a claim true.

"The pack came from the club bin," she said.

There is no club bin.

CHAPTER 5

Timer Check

The back hall keeps its own weather. Cooler air. Dust that minds its manners. Machines that do not care about anyone's feelings.

I took Asa to the breaker first. He read labels without touching them. Main. Front bay. Rare nook. Stockroom line. Wall timer. Each toggle sat where Rafi left it. Straight as soldiers.

"Wheel," Asa said.

Rafi opened the metal cover on the wall dial. The new wheel we installed last fall stared back, clean white, black pins. The ON tab sat locked in the always-on slot. The ring of little trip pins showed none pressed down. The small red hand that marks next cut pointed at nothing. We had defeated the dial before tonight and left it there. A person could still flip the switch under it, but the wheel would not schedule anything by itself.

"Dial is off," Rafi said. "Has been all night. I checked at five and nine. I did not touch it at midnight."

"Good," Asa said.

Havel looked at the face, sniffed the casing the way he sometimes does when cheap electronics burn. No heat. No scent. He nodded.

"Router next," I said.

We moved one step down to the cabinet. A tidy rack for a small shop. Modem, router, hub for the smart bulbs, a UPS that keeps our memory when the grid burps. I slid the cabinet door, hit the admin bookmark on the shop tablet, and entered our long password from a card behind plastic. Rafi stood by my shoulder. He knows these screens, but I log the act when the room is like this.

"Dashboard," I said. "Peppermint Cat Guest active. Five leases issued tonight, devices present since before eleven. No new joins during the blackout."

"As expected," Asa said. "Event log."

I navigated to the syslog. The page filled with the quiet gossip of a network. DHCP leases. Connects. Disconnects. A line every few seconds with a time code. Rafi scrolled to 23:50. We read downward together.

23:56:12 AP FrontBay disassoc client iPhone-JR.
23:56:21 AP FrontBay assoc client iPhone-JR RSSI -59.
23:58:03 AP FrontBay assoc client Benji's-Phone RSSI -63.
23:59:54 HueHub group Lights pre-stage OFF from device ME-TAB.
00:00:00 HueHub group Lights OFF command from device ME-TAB.
00:00:01 AP FrontBay beacon interval stable.
00:00:02 HueHub group Lights pre-stage ON from device ME-TAB.
00:00:05 HueHub group Lights ON command from device ME-TAB.
00:00:06 AP FrontBay disassoc client none.
00:05:00 HueHub group Lights OFF command from device ME-TAB.
00:05:02 HueHub group Lights ON command from device ME-TAB.

Rafi tapped the two lines that mattered. "We run Philips smart bulbs in the bay," he said for the record. "They ride the Hue hub.

The wall dial does not control them. The Hue logs show a pre-stage at 23:59:54 and the OFF at 00:00:00. Then an ON a few seconds after. Group name Lights. Device label ME-TAB."

"Who is ME-TAB," Asa said, already knowing the answer he wanted.

"Device naming shows up under DHCP leases and under cached clients," I said. "Guest network lists familiar nicknames. My phone. Rafi's laptop when we test public logins. Last week a tablet tagged ME-TAB associated. Not tonight. But the hub hears device names even when the app issues a cloud command through our bridge. It logs the label the app presents."

Rafi flipped to the DHCP lease table and the known devices list. He pointed to last week's Tuesday. "Cached client," he read. "ME-TAB. Vendor string shows Samsung. MAC A0:2B:3C:1D:EE:90. First seen three Thursdays ago at Book Club Live, last seen last week during Poetry Night. Associated to Peppermint Cat Guest both times."

"Print that," Asa said.

Rafi hit print. The little laser on the counter in front chirped and spat a page. Peppermint watched it like prey and then decided dignity outweighed sport.

I scrolled to the Hue hub's own log. Its web panel prints in a blunt way I trust.

23:59:54 Scene prepare OFF by user ME-TAB on group 1 Lights.
00:00:00 OFF by user ME-TAB on group 1 Lights.
00:00:05 ON by user ME-TAB on group 1 Lights.
00:05:00 OFF by user ME-TAB on group 1 Lights.
00:05:02 ON by user ME-TAB on group 1 Lights.

"Zeroed to midnight," I said. "Not the wall dial. Not the breaker. A straight command from the app bound to our hub. Device name ME-TAB."

Havel made two small ticks on his pad. He does not need a speech when a log prints the speech for him.

"Asa," I said, "the OFF at five past."

"Someone tested their power once they liked the first result," he said. "Or someone checked their toy. Either way, it did not cause the thud."

Rafi backed out to the AP client list and pointed to the connected devices during the hour. "iPhone-JR," he read. "That is Jenna when she forgets to rename. She associated at 23:56 and stayed. Benji's phone came and went. Conrad's did not join. Erica's stayed with Guest from earlier. Margo's phone name hides on Bluetooth as ME-Phone when she pairs to the speaker, but on Wi-Fi she leaves it as iPhone. I have seen both."

"ME-TAB," Asa said. "Not iPhone. Tablet."

Rafi nodded. "She brought a tablet sleeve into the room," he said. "I saw it. Liora saw it."

"I did," I said. "She called it minutes."

Asa looked at the wheel again as if to give it a chance to tell him a new story. It stayed dumb. Good.

"Photograph the panel screens," he said. "Hue hub with the midnight OFF and ON. Router syslog with the same. DHCP table showing ME-TAB last seen last week on Guest. Cached client list with the vendor string. Label Peppermint Cat Guest visible in the header."

I took each shot with the shop tablet's camera so the file shows the context. Today's paper taped at the edge of the screen for anchor, scale card on the bezel, my hand not in frame. Old habit. Good habit.

Rafi printed the Hue hub log page and the AP event slice. He stapled the prints to two fresh evidence cards. I wrote the lines. Hue hub confirms OFF and ON at 00:00:00 and 00:00:05, group Lights, user ME-TAB. Router syslog shows same times. Guest SSID Peppermint Cat Guest.

We bagged the prints because a defense attorney once tried to say a screenshot is theater. Paper with a chain makes theater cry.

"Asa," Havel said, "ask her for the tablet."

"In a minute," Asa said. "I want one more look at the route from the wheel to the bay. Liora, tell me how the power flows."

"Breaker feeds the bay outlets and the Hue hub through the UPS," I said. "The wall dial controls the old fluorescent line in the stockroom only. We replaced front bay strips last year with smart bulbs because the ballast hummed like a dying bee. The dial has nothing to do with those bulbs. The app speaks to the hub. The hub tells the bulbs to go dark. Anyone can push the app if they have the bridge on their account and our network or a cloud path."

"Can a person not on your Wi-Fi still push the command," Havel said.

"Yes," Rafi said. "If they paired their app to our bridge when they were on our Wi-Fi before. The app remembers the bridge and can send commands through the vendor's cloud. The hub logs the command with the device name the app supplies. It does not care whether the device is joined to Wi-Fi right now."

"So the tablet did not need to be on Guest at midnight," Asa said. "It only needed to know our bridge and have an internet path."

"Correct," Rafi said. "And the log tells you who."

I opened the Hue app on our own admin phone to make one last control. I toggled a test group for the stockroom lamp twice. The router wrote the events at 00:36:12 and 00:36:13. It recorded Liora-Admin. The hub wrote Liora-Admin. Good. The place tells on all of us with equal rude honesty.

"Wheel stays off," I said, touching its case with one knuckle so the camera could see the lack of movement. "No pins down. Red hand pointing at nothing. Twice checked. Rafi did not touch it at midnight."

"Confirm that verbally," Asa said.

"I did not touch the dial at midnight," Rafi said. "I was at the hall mouth, two steps from the circle, and I stopped when Liora said hold. I checked the router log, not the wheel."

We returned to the floor with the prints. The circle still held because I had told it to. Jenna sat with her tote on her knees like a child holding a toy she knows will be taken. Conrad had turned his chair one degree away from the aisle, a tiny cheat the room would remember. Benji held his water and did not drink. Margo had her hands in her lap and her chin angled for sympathy.

Asa set the prints on the lockbox table and spoke like a judge doing the kind part of a bad day.

"Margo," he said. "At 23:59:54 a device labeled ME-TAB sent a pre-stage OFF to our smart bulb group named Lights. At midnight it sent OFF. At 00:00:05 it sent ON. At 00:05:00 it sent OFF again. At 00:05:02 it sent ON. Our wall timer wheel was set to always on. The breaker was not touched. This is app control."

She smiled too quickly. "It must be my house app," she said. "I sometimes check my lamps when I get nervous. It settles me."

"You live on Fir," I said. "Your home network does not carry the name Peppermint Cat Guest."

She kept the smile but the eyes went dull for half a second. "What does your network have to do with my lamps," she said.

Rafi slid the cached devices print toward her without reaching too far. He does not taunt. He presents.

"Your tablet has been on our Guest network before," he said. "Label ME-TAB. Your phone is ME-Phone when you pair to the speaker. Your tablet knows our bridge because you paired it here last week. When you push your app, it sees the Peppermint Cat hub and offers it as a choice. You chose it tonight. The hub logs ME-TAB. Your house lamps did not dim. Ours did."

Jenna made the face of someone watching a fight they wish they had taped. She pressed her lips together to keep joy from showing. She is not good at that.

"I do not know what any of that means," Margo said. "I am not technical. I only wanted a soft moment at midnight. You know, to make the vote feel ceremonial."

"There was no vote," I said. "There was a fall."

"The lamp dip did not kill anyone," she said.

"It made dark," Asa said. "Dark made movement. Movement made a ladder tip. We will measure the rest."

She stared at his pen as if it had called her stupid. She met my eyes. She tried to find a version of me who would sell her a way out. Not tonight.

Havel spoke now, calm and precise. "The part you own is the choice to toggle another person's room without consent," he said. "You used an app with a cached bridge on a network labeled Peppermint Cat Guest. You staged a blackout at midnight in a circle that had said no."

"That is not a crime," she said. "It was a theatrical gesture."

"Tonight it is evidence," he said.

Asa turned to me. "Put a card on the wheel," he said. "Timer wheel verified always on. No pin changes. No odor of heat. No handprints added since five."

I wrote the card and stuck it with painter's tape to the metal access door. We would swab later if anyone begged forensics to find sweat on a cheap dial. I was not wasting swabs on that.

"Put a card on the hub," he said. "Hue hub shows OFF and ON from ME-TAB at midnight and five past. Guest SSID visible. Admin page photographed. DHCP shows cached client ME-TAB last week."

I wrote it and taped it to the cabinet door. I added the time. 00:38. I signed. Rafi signed under me. Havel initialed the edge. The camera took one more of me with the card for later when memory gets argumentative.

We kept the prints on the table with the ballot stack photos. Peppermint sniffed them both, decided nothing smelled like fish, and returned to the warm spot by the receipt printer.

Jenna raised her hand again as if a teacher would save her. "Does this mean I did not cause the fall," she said.

"It means your part has its own box," Asa said. "We will open it next."

Conrad cracked his knuckles like a man who needs to hear his own body make a noise he can control. "Vote should stand," he said to no one. "We came to do governance."

"You came to run someone out before she finished a sentence," I said. "You missed."

He flinched.

Benji stared at the Hue log and looked relieved to have something he could treat like a library record. "The device name gives the owner away," he said. "That is clean."

"It is," I said. "When people name their toys with their initials, rooms get honest."

Margo straightened her blazer hem again, tug by tug, as if fabric could behave where facts would not. "You cannot prove ME is me," she said.

"We will match the MAC," Rafi said. "When we get your tablet."

"Which you are not getting," she said.

Asa smiled without joy. "We will get it," he said. "You can hand it to me or I can get it with paper. Pick the method that respects your night."

She swallowed and looked back toward the ballots and then toward the aisle, which finally had learned how to go quiet.

I looked up at the wall clock for the camera and for the habit. "Time zero forty," I said. "Wheel verified. Hub log photographed. Router log printed. Device label ME-TAB tied to Peppermint Cat Guest. Rafi did not touch the dial at midnight."

The camera on the counter does not care about tone. It only writes light to a card. Good. We would need all of it when the morning wanted its own story and the chamber tried to put a ribbon on a trick.

Margo tried one last sentence. "My app controls my house lamps," she said. "If your lights responded, it is because your network listens."

"Wrong network," I said. "Our hub listens to commands that your device sent to it. Your app does not control my house. It controlled my shop. That is the point."

She closed her mouth. She had run out of ways to pretend this part belonged to somebody else.

Asa tapped the printed Hue log with his pen. "We can move," he said to Havel. "Wheel is out. App is in. Next we fix the chair path and the audio."

Havel nodded. He wrote one more line on his pad. He does not fill paper to look busy. He writes the part that pays.

We left the back hall with the time stated and the cards stuck and the printouts bagged. The room waited. The ladder kept its pose. The ballot stack sat in sleeves. The timer phone pulsed one greener ring for no one's benefit.

The night had chosen its methods. We were choosing ours.

CHAPTER 6

Chair Scrape

The circle looked harmless from a distance. Eight chairs, one rug, one low table with a lockbox that behaved. Up close the floor read like a ruled page. Weight had written on it during the cut.

"We mark the path," Asa said.

"Start with the skew," I said.

Jenna's chair still sat crooked. Not a small angle. A turn of three hands on the clock face, nose pointed at the lockbox and the near end of the travel shelf, tail away from the alley door. I crouched, set the scale card at the front foot, and took a shot that caught the arc pressed into the rug. Fibers leaned with the push, not with any pull toward the exit.

"Direction points to the box, not the door," I said. "Whoever moved here did not aim for air."

Rafi brought the thin chalk I keep for floor grids. Not to write over clues. To frame them. I traced the pale bend the chair had carved, a curve that clipped the corner of the low table and stopped shy of the aisle mouth. The gouge in the foot pad showed raw rubber. Fresh. Clean edges. A ragged thread of carpet fiber clung to it. I photographed the pad, then the thread. I spoke the time for both.

"Time zero forty-two," I said. "Skew angle recorded. Front foot shows fresh abrasion. Arc points toward ballot box."

Havel stood two paces back, eyes on the chair back, not the feet. "Blue," he said.

I followed his look. A hair-thin sliver of yarn clung to the top rail of the chair back, right where a shoulder would ride when a person shoved past in tight quarters. Pale, close to robin's egg. Erica's cardigan owned that color. I did not touch it.

"Tweezers," I said.

Rafi opened the kit and held them out with a small glassine. I steadied my breath and lifted the fiber like it might break. It behaved. I set it in the envelope and pinned the flap with a clip so the static would not win.

"Pale blue fiber from chair back," I said. "Position top rail, right side. Likely transfer when someone brushed past Erica's seat in the blackout. Time zero forty-three."

Asa angled his head. "Photograph the seat backs in the ring," he said. "If this one shows a single transfer, the others will give us context."

I walked the circle. Back rails clean on five. One more faint lint on Benji's chair, not blue, not near the rail edge, older fuzz that reads as room life. Only this one showed a fresh blue that matched what lay at the endcap.

"One fiber is not a fortune," Havel said, mild. "But the path loves it."

"It tells us where the body had to be when the press past happened," I said. "Erica sat here. Blue caught here. Chair turned toward the box, not toward the alley. The move was in, not out."

Conrad snorted. "Or she stood," he said. "You're stretching rug marks like taffy."

"Her hands were on her knees," I said. "She said it. The room heard it. The fiber does not care what we want. It sits where it sits."

Asa lifted the chair by its back with two fingers under the rail and tilted it a hair. He does not like scraping clues across rugs. He checked the rear feet. No fresh abrasion. Only the front foot told a story.

"This was not a small scoot," he said. "This was a grab and twist."

"From where," Havel said.

We stood where bodies had sat. I took Erica's chair and held my palms open. Rafi took Jenna's seat and set his toes where hers had been. Asa pointed a knuckle at the angle.

"On the cut," he said, "someone puts a hand to the right shoulder here, shoves, and reaches past the back rail toward the center. Chair pivots left, toward the table. The person who did the shove moves inward. The person in this chair flinches. Blue goes to wood. Then the thud."

I pictured the breathy no we had heard. The arc matched the word.

"Ballot motive," Havel said.

"Or box cover," I said. "Either way the vector does not walk to the exit."

Rafi took a lint roller sheet and patted the air a hair above the chair back to catch whatever else the rail wanted to give without stripping it. One more pale filament lifted and clung to the sheet. He pressed it to a second glassine and folded twice.

"Two fibers," he said. "Same hue. Close twist. We can match to the cardigan when Asa is done with photos on the aisle."

We logged both envelopes with clean hands. I slid them into a pouch with a thin card that gave the seat location in short words. Havel signed the edge.

Jenna watched like a person reading her own subpoena. "I did not touch Erica," she said.

"Your chair tells on you in a different way," I said. "We will get to that."

She shut her mouth for once.

I moved back to the rug and used the chalk to mark the scrape's start. I took a second photo with the lockbox in frame. The low table had a narrow scuff on the leg closest to the path. New, silver at the bite. I set the scale card by it and shot again.

"Impact on table leg," I said. "Grain shows a raw nick. Height matches the skewed chair's seat rail."

Rafi fished the small rubber foot cap box from under the counter. We replace those monthly because people drag furniture even when asked not to. He matched the diameter of the gouged pad to the empty slot in the box lid and wrote that on a line. He likes dimensions. He is right to.

"Asa," I said, "you want the route on a single overhead."

"Yes," he said. "Give me a bird's eye. Skew, chalk curve, box, table, aisle mouth."

I stood on the step stool, set the shop phone to wide, held my breath and snapped. Twice for luck. Once with today's paper clipped to the rug by a binder clip so the date lived in the frame. No glamour. Meals for a judge.

"The scrape tells you where a body moved in the cut," I said. "The fiber tells you who the body met."

Havel looked at the alley door and then back at Conrad. "This points away from the exit," he said.

Conrad did not answer. He measured the door again.

Asa knelt by Jenna's chair and followed the chalk mark with his finger without touching the rug. He stopped at a spot where the arc kinked inward. "Second hand on the back," he said. "Or a foot catching the leg. The path jumps a finger toward the box here."

"Try it," I said.

He set two fingers on the rail of an empty chair and gave it a short shove. The front foot found the rug nap in the same angle and hopped the way the kink showed. He nodded. "Hands, not hips," he said. "This is not a person standing up in a clean line. This is a person pushed."

Jenna exhaled and caught it. "I stood to grab my tote," she said. "That is what the chair shows."

"Your tote did not sit on the table," I said. "It sat on your knees. This marks a forward twist with pressure at the back. A hand. Not your own."

Margo raised her chin. "None of this proves a shove," she said. "Chairs move in rooms. People stand. We had a blackout. I asked for ceremony. We got chaos."

"You asked for leverage," Erica would have said if she could still speak. I said it for her. "You staged a dip at the bell. Hands moved where the path gave room. People who know rooms know how to write lines in rugs. You know rooms."

Margo tried a new face. Sympathetic. Tired. Responsible. It convinced no one, not even her.

I knelt at Erica's chair and looked at the right back post where shoulder meets wood. No dent. No blood. Only the pale threads. The cardigan's knit would give fibers with one sharp brush. I knew that yarn. I bought it for the shop wrap we keep for customers who forget coats. Erica had loved the color and found the same dye lot. I had written the receipt myself.

"You find meaning in lint," Conrad said, trying on a smirk.

"I find timing in lint," I said. "Transfer lives within seconds. This did not ride over from another night. It landed at midnight and ten heartbeats. It leans the way a shove leans. Toward the box, not the door."

He rolled his eyes at the ceiling. It looks like stone when men do it. It looks like fear when the room answers.

Rafi set a fresh path card at the edge of the rug with an arrow that matched the chalk. He labeled it Chair vector to box, not exit. He does not decorate. He prints what we will need in a week when the story tries to change its shoes.

Asa pointed at the lockbox. "Key," he said.

Rafi opened his palm and showed it. He had not let it go. He set it on the counter next to the timer phone tray and stepped back. The camera caught the key, the box, the chalk path, and the skewed chair in one frame. Asa took the shot himself. He does not outsource moments that matter.

Havel had watched the floor. Now he watched faces. "Who sat where," he said.

I pointed. "Erica here. Jenna here, skewed. Margo behind me. Benji left. Conrad left of Benji. I stood here. Rafi at the hall mouth."

Havel wrote initials on a small index of seats. He drew an arrow along the chalk line and drew a small cross at the kink. He put a tiny dot on the chair back where the fiber had clung. I like his maps. They look like recipes.

"Call the time," Asa said.

"Time zero forty-seven," I said. "Chair scrape marked. Path toward the ballot box, not the exit. Fresh gouge on front foot. Table leg nicked along the line. Pale blue fiber on Erica's chair back, top rail, right side. Two threads bagged."

Peppermint hopped down from the counter as if the sentence bored him and strolled to the chalk mark. He sniffed, sneezed once, and stepped over the line like a cat with respect for boundaries. He took the moderator seat and turned twice before sitting. No one laughed.

"Do you think the shove happened before the ladder swung," Benji said. He had that tone people get when they try to be useful without pushing their luck.

"Yes," I said. "Audio next will fix the order. But the arc shows movement at the start of the cut. I heard the chair skid before the thud."

Jenna flinched. She had heard it too. Her eyes went to the tote. She could not stop them. Asa watched the vector of her glance as if it were another chalk line.

Conrad cracked his knuckles again. "Vote should stand," he said. "We took the time. It was planned. We should see it through."

55

"Your cousin lies at the endcap," I said. "The only plan left is the one that keeps faith with the room."

He looked at the back door instead of me. His jaw worked. His heel marked the rug with a nervous tap. Havel looked down and saw the new dot his shoe had pressed. He wrote it with the grace of a man who knows when to let small tells hang in the air.

Asa capped his pen. "We have enough on this piece," he said. "Path in. Not out. Transfer. We will knit it to the audio and the hub log. Then we ask for the tablet."

Margo watched the door like Conrad did now. The change in her face landed as a click. People who sell nights know when a night stops buying. She stiffened and reached for posture to carry her across the gap. It made her look taller. It did not make her safer.

I looked at the board in my head, now with new lines. Ballots with a mark out of time. A wheel ruled out. An app labeled with initials that match a mouth. A chair that sprang toward the box and kissed a table. A fiber that went from a blue sleeve to wood when the room went dark. The path was not elegant. It did not need to be.

I took one last photo of the chalk curve with the lockbox and the tablet sleeve's zipper peeking from Margo's tote in the same plane. I forced the light to behave and give me a clean depth on both. It would pay when someone at a desk asked where intent sits on a floor.

"Time zero forty-nine," I said for the camera, the room, and the night that would not want to be remembered. "Chair scrape recorded. Vector toward box. Fiber logged. Table nick logged."

Conrad snapped like a man who wants to get ahead of a tide.

"The vote should stand," he said again. "City needs order."

He watched the door when he said it. Not the aisle. Not the box. The door.

CHAPTER 7

Cousin Angle

The office sits six steps up from the floor and prints the truth if you ask in the right order. I led Asa and Havel through the staff gate, past the returns cart, and into the glass box where the safe hums and the old laser waits to show its receipts.

Rafi took the chair by the desktop and woke the monitor. He had the club chat tab ready because he knows where nights go. Peppermint came with us without being invited, sprang to the file cabinet, then to the window ledge, then to the top of the bookshelf where the staplers live like small blue dogs. He stared at the blinking cursor like it owed him money.

"Two folders," I said. "Club chat captures and printer logs. We do the chat first. Then we tie it to paper."

Havel stood behind Rafi's shoulder but left him a clear line. Asa took the corner spot by the safe and pulled his notebook without opening it yet. He watches screens the way other people watch fish tanks, calm, critical, never fooled by the water.

Rafi opened the chat archive. The club lives on one of those free platforms that strips privacy down to a slogan and gives you a sticker. We run screenshots for anything we care about. I had asked Talia to set the bot last month when Margo floated the word procedure. Tonight paid off that small habit.

I took the mouse. "Filter," I said. "User Margo. Last thirty days."

Dates and lines rolled into view. Margo writes like a person who thinks short posts are icing on a party cake. Tonight those sprinkles lined up in a row.

I clicked the thread from two days ago. Margo, 10:06, in the club chat: "Proposal for next meeting: introduce a procedural vote to confirm moderator role for the next quarter. Language: Midnight Reading Club Procedural Vote, Moderator, Keep or Remove. Simple majority. Paper ballots to protect feelings." Under it a graphic mock-up with the header exactly as printed on the stack downstairs. Same dull serif. Same line breaks. A tiny cat icon in the upper right that our chamber template adds because some designer won a fight in a committee five years ago.

"Read it," Asa said.

I did, out loud. "Proposal, introduce procedural vote, confirm moderator, Keep or Remove. Paper ballots to protect feelings. Language matches the printed header."

Rafi dragged in a second window with the photo we shot of the ballot header at the counter. We tiled them. They married. I did not need to say it. The room saw it.

"Scroll," Havel said.

We dropped to the earlier thread where Conrad had posted a rent memo. He does that when he wants to take a temperature before he feeds a draft to the chamber. This one dated a week back. Title: "Revised Mixed-Use Leases, Peppermint Block." His note: "Early share for feedback, this aligns with chamber revitalization goals." It listed stepped increases and an "activation plan" that would turn the upstairs storage into event space with a surcharge for after-hours bookings. I know that language. It reads like a fire trying to wear a tie.

Erica replied four minutes later with a link to a tenant group message that she wrote and we co-signed last month. "Opposed," she wrote in chat. "These increases violate the cap we negotiated. The activation plan encroaches on quiet hours and would put costs on tenants who need stability, not events. Expect a formal block at the council session. We will come with names."

Below that she posted screenshots of signatures and a list of tenants ready to show up. The screenshot carried the council stamp from the intake desk. Date and time on it matched the night she and I stood under cold fluorescent light while the clerk checked our forms twice and stapled them with the kind of care I trust.

Conrad's response a minute later in the chat: "Let's keep this civil." Then, "We can revisit moderators next quarter."

Seven minutes after that Margo chimed in with the key line again. "Procedural vote next meeting. Moderator confirmation. Paper ballots. Midnight for a clean reset." The graphic returned. Same header. Same words.

I scrolled further back. Margo used the phrase "Protect feelings" twice more across the months. She likes that mask. She puts it on when she wants to hit someone and not leave a bruise people can see from the sidewalk.

"Screen cap the run," Asa said. "Include the timestamp column."

Rafi hit the capture tool and saved a strip: Conrad's rent memo, Erica's block with the council stamp, Margo's repeated ballot language. He printed it to PDF and named it something boring a clerk will not sneer at. ClubChat_Run_Conrad_Erica_Margo_30d.pdf. He moved it to a folder that our backup hits every hour and then exported a flat image for the chain binder. He does three copies when the night wants to grow teeth.

"Now the queue," I said.

We switched from chat to printer history. The cheap laser does not forget who fed it. It keeps a job list with titles, users, start times, page counts. If you do not clear the log, it will serve you later when a person claims an empty hand.

Rafi had not cleared it. Bless him. The queue showed

tonight's receipts, a stack of bookmarks for the kid program, and then one entry at 10:02 p.m. User: FrontDesk. Document: MRC_Procedural_Vote_Moderator.pdf. Pages: 25. Status: Completed. Duplex: No. Source: USB. The job size lined up with a short PDF, single sheet printed multiple times. Time stamp made sense. That hit while the shop had a quiet lull between dinner and the club.

"Who printed at 10:02," Havel said.

"FrontDesk is the shop profile," Rafi said. "Talia had the desk then. I was in the back waxing the travel aisle. Liora did a stock count. Talia would not queue a PDF with that title on her own."

"We confirm," Asa said. "Pull the spool file if it lives."

Rafi tapped into the print server cache. The job had dropped its shadow file into the temporary folder, not the spool, but he had set the system to hold the last three. The filepath sat fresh. He clicked open. The PDF title bar at the top of the viewer read MRC_Procedural_Vote_Moderator.pdf. The document properties showed Author: M. Ellsworth, Created: 21:58, Modified: 22:01, Application: Preview, Producer: Quartz PDFContext.

"Screen," I said.

We captured the properties pane with the title, author, and created time. We captured the print queue with the 10:02 job. We captured the desktop clock in the corner to anchor our own time. We printed those captures, then labeled the prints with a line across the bottom. Printer queue confirms PDF job at 10:02 p.m. Title matches ballot header language. Author metadata M. Ellsworth. Pages printed 25. I signed. Asa signed. Rafi initialed, because he touched the mouse.

"Source of the PDF," Asa said. "Where did it save from."

"Downloads shows a save at 22:01 by FrontDesk," Rafi said. He opened the folder. One file with the same title sat there. He clicked it. The viewer showed the same header as our paper stack downstairs. The tiny cat icon sat smug in the corner. The watermark did not appear on screen, of course. That lives in paper. The text did.

"USB source in the print log," Havel said.

"Flash drive," I said. "Someone brought the PDF on a stick, handed it to Talia, and asked for a run. Or handed it to Margo's friend sitting nearby. Either way the machine says the document lived on a drive, not in our cloud."

Rafi clicked the little arrow on the print job's details. The path read /Volumes/UNTITLED/MRC_Procedural_Vote_Moderator.pdf. That is as anonymous as a thief. He pulled the list of recently mounted volumes. It showed UNTITLED at 21:59, EJECTED at 22:03.

"Camera on the counter at that hour," Asa said.

"Front bay points the wrong way," I said. "It gets the door and the wall clock. It does not see the USB slot. My nose says Talia would have shouted if she felt used. She did not. I will ask her in the morning with coffee and the copy of the queue. She will remember who stood at the desk at 21:59."

Havel nodded. He trusts clerks. He was one before he learned to carry a badge.

I pulled up Margo's chat again and opened a post from last week where she practiced lines. "Ballots keep the room calm," she wrote then. "No faces. No pressure. Outcome without spectacle." The exact phrase outcome without spectacle rode under tonight's header too, in small text no one reads unless they stare. I enlarged both. They matched, period for period.

"PDF title matches printed header," I said. "Chat language matches the small line. She rehearsed in public. Then she printed in my office."

Asa raised his eyebrows an inch. "That part reads plain," he said.

We exported the PDF properties as a text file and stapled it to the printout. I logged the file path and the volume name on a card and tucked the card into the sleeve with the print queue capture. I made a quick note for myself for dawn. Ask Talia the four questions. Who handed you a stick. What color. Where did they stand. What did they say to present it as harmless. That fourth one always matters. People sell tricks with a tone.

Peppermint made a soft chirp that meant he wanted to be remembered. He stretched, dropped from the cabinet to the desk, walked across the keyboard without shame, and sat on the printer with his paws tucked like a loaf. He looked smug. He always looks smug.

I opened Erica's tenant group messages and printed the one with the council stamp again so the chain had a copy that did not only live inside the chat strip. The header on that message showed the clerk's initials in the corner. The rent cap part read simple enough that a sponsor would understand it. That sentence is a gift. I circled it with a pen. Not for evidence. For my own head. Motive sits better on paper when it has a sentence you cannot wriggle past.

Conrad's memo in the chat, "revitalization goals," lined up clean against Erica's block. Margo's ballot language arrived within ten minutes of that block. All three lived in the same feed. Screenshots capture that adjacency. It says planning without needing anyone to confess.

"Now the chamber copier," Asa said. "We know the ghost ring. We know the watermark. We know the queue and the USB stick. This bridge ties to that bridge."

"We close that tomorrow in daylight," I said. "The clerk will let me photograph the glass, because she hates that ring as much as I do. I will take a test copy of a blank and match the nick to our bottom sheet. If she says no, Len will call her at lunch with a story about how much money she saved the gallery with one simple swab. She likes Len."

Havel made a face that passed for a smile. "Do your museum dance later," he said. "Tonight we fix motive."

We returned to chat. I filtered by Erica's name and showed the list of her posts in the club over the last three months. She had built the tenant roster for our block in the open. She had set meeting dates in this feed. She had posted legal links for rent caps with line numbers. She had not once posted a party photo with a caption about vibes. She had asked people to bring ledgers. She had asked people to sign their names in ink. People like that stop rooms from being stolen.

"Conrad's plan died because she made the room pay attention," I said.

"She made him lose money," Havel said. "He is family, he is landlord, and he hates that she learned how to use a stamp."

"Family payback hides inside calls for process," I said. "People excuse a shove if a ballot rides its shoulders."

Asa wrote three words. Rent, ballot, timing. He does not write poetry. He writes pegs for the board.

Rafi clicked the local print server's job history again and pulled a CSV export. He added it to the evidence folder with a boring name, because boring sticks. He did not gloat about the author field on the PDF. He is not that kind of person.

"Pull Margo's posts with the graphic," Asa said. "All of them. We shoot them side by side with the ballot header downstairs."

I did. Rafi printed the strip, laid it on the desk, and I set the ballot header print next to it. Same line breaks. Same thin rule under the header. Same transform on the cat icon. I photographed that pair with the scale card and today's paper and signed the back of the photo when it came out because some judge thirty months from now will ask who shot this and I will be old enough to want to answer without pain.

"Next," Havel said.

"Printer preferences," Rafi said. "Sometimes the PDF metadata carries a document ID in the headers that shows the original title before export. Then you catch people who change file names to hide a trail."

He cracked the print spool file with a hex viewer. He scrolled to the PostScript header. It showed Title: Midnight Reading Club Procedural Vote, Moderator. Author: M. Ellsworth. CreateDate:

2024-04-14 21:58:13. Producer: Quartz. No renames. Clean and dumb. He grinned, not for the room, for himself. He loves when files tell the truth without being coaxed.

"Print that header," Asa said.

We did. It looked like nonsense to anyone who had not run a desktop in the early two thousands, and like a confession to anyone who had.

"Who touched the USB," Havel said.

"I will pull the counter cam anyway," I said. "It faces the clock, not the port, but it might catch a hand with a drive and a sleeve color. And we ring the chamber desk in the morning and ask who slipped in late to run a stack. The clerk sees everybody who abuses her copier. She maintains a list in her head. She will say a name before she knows she has said it."

Asa closed his notebook. He does that when a section is done. "We take this down to the counter," he said. "We pair it with the ballots and the hub log and the chair path. Then we ask for the tablet."

"One more," I said, holding up a finger without playing teacher. "Erica's block killed the rent plan. The ballot language appears minutes after. Margo's graphic matches the printed header. The PDF metadata matches her initials. The print queue hits at 10:02. The source reads USB. The chamber copier stamps a coffee ring on exactly where our blank shows a ghost. Add in the watermark from Gran's ream that ran out last summer, which Gran confirms. That stack came from one person with access to our back and the chamber machine, and that person rehearsed in public."

Havel nodded. "That sentence can go in a warrant," he said.

Peppermint made a new noise, the one he uses when a drawer calls him by name. He leaped from the printer to the desk, put a paw on my office keys, and in one arrogant sweep flicked the chain toward the ledge. The big brass office key slid under the corner shelf and vanished into the inch of dust that waits to collect a debt. Peppermint looked pleased with himself, then bored, then sleepy.

Rafi started to laugh and clapped a hand over his mouth. Asa looked at the gap under the shelf and then at me like a man who deserves better from cats. Havel shook his head. The world had given us one ounce of comedy without permission. We took it.

"Not a clue," I said. "Only a cat."

"Still goes in my book," Asa said. "To keep me honest when this night starts to feel larger than it is."

I crouched, reached an arm into the gap, and caught nothing but dust and a single receipt that had fallen under there sometime in late winter. Peppermint peered down and tapped my wrist with soft claws like he wanted to referee. I pulled my arm back, stood, and glared without heat.

"Use the spare," Rafi said. He handed me the red-tagged key from the hook. He marked the loss on the pegboard and wrote a small note that said cat put it there and drew a tiny crown over the word cat. He cannot help himself.

We packed the printouts into sleeves. I slid the chat strip behind the ballot photos and tucked the PDF properties behind the queue capture. I kept the ghost ring in its own pouch and put a copy of the chat graphic next to it so the header lived with the ring. Files keep secrets unless you seat them next to their friends.

We stepped back to the floor. The circle stayed quiet. The aisle stayed sealed. The lockbox stayed shut. The timer phone pulsed its green ring like a heart that belonged to a bad plan. Conrad watched the door as if fresh air would give him an alibi. Margo watched the table where the ballots had sat as if paper forgives.

I set the chat strip on the counter and anchored it with the scale card and the half-inch of my palm that says pay attention. I set the print queue capture beside it and the PDF properties under it. I laid the ballot header print across both like a bridge. I did not look at Margo when I spoke.

"Erica blocked the rent plan," I said. "You moved for a secret ballot to get her out of the moderator seat. You printed the stack at ten with a file that carries your initials. You fed marked stock through the chamber copier with a ghost ring on its glass. Your tablet tossed the lights. The chair turned toward the box. The fiber says who took the shove. The ladder says what hit the floor."

No one applauded. Good. The shop does not clap for work it expects.

Conrad's mouth opened. He closed it. He tried again and pulled out the only thing he had left.

"The vote should stand," he said. He watched the door while he said it. He did not watch the aisle. He did not watch the stack. He watched a way out.

CHAPTER 8

Pod Tape

We took the back table. No audience. One lamp. One recorder. The shop felt smaller here, which is how I like it when truth needs a desk.

Jenna set her tote down as if it were fragile and valuable. It was neither. She lifted out her phone and kept a finger on it like someone who knows that handing over a device can end a career you built on clips.

"You said you captured room ambience," Asa said. "We need the raw."

"It's clean," she said. "No edits. It'll help you fix time."

"It will help us fix you," Asa said. "Airplane mode. Unlock it. Put it on the table."

She blinked. She did it. The satisfaction of that small click lived in the quiet like a coin in a jar.

Rafi brought the shop laptop, the short cable, two clean drives, and a notepad with the chain card clipped to it. He does chain the way other people do prayer.

"Voice Memos or video," I said.

"Voice," Jenna said. "Lossless setting."

"Name of the file," Asa said.

She scrolled. "Roombed_0414," she said, proud of the cute.

Rafi did not smile. He plugged in. The phone asked to trust. Jenna tapped Allow with a reluctant thumb. He pulled the file into a new folder on the shop drive named PCT_0414_Audio_JR. He copied the same file to the second drive for a mirror. He ran a checksum on both copies and read the hash out loud while I wrote it. He set both drives in sleeves and labeled them with the date, time, and initials. He handed one to Asa. He slid the other into the lockbox with the evidence cards and shut the lid.

"Airplane mode stays on," Asa said. "Do not touch your cloud."

Jenna looked offended and then remembered the room she occupied. She kept both hands on her knees. Good.

Rafi opened the file on the shop laptop. The waveform laid itself out across the screen in blue. Sixteen minutes and change. He turned the volume low and handed me the headphones. I put them on. They smelled like the box they live in. Dry foam and cable.

"Before we play," Asa said, "state the position of the phone during the recording."

"In my chair, on my lap," Jenna said. "I wanted true circle tone."

"You never set it down," Asa said.

"No," she said. "Lap the whole time."

Rafi typed the sentence under the file name. He added the words claimed lap position, continuous.

"Run it," I said.

He hit space. The room came up in my ears, smaller and tighter than it felt live. The first two minutes were our voices, low, trading pages. A steady hiss sat under everything, low and smooth. Not the fridge by the counter. That unit has a tired fan with a small pulse. This bed sounded like the HVAC branch over the travel shelf. I make that sound in my sleep when a tour group decides the stack wants heat.

At 23:56 the file caught Rafi's test chime. One ping with the polite echo this room gives low brass. The HV branch hiss slipped for a second when the damper checked itself. It does that once in a while on nights like this when the outside air decides the shop needs attention. Jenna had not sat under that branch. The phone had.

"Not lap in the circle," I said. "This bed sits near the travel shelf. HVAC signature from that vent. The fridge does not sing on this bed."

"Your fridge sings," Jenna said, trying for light.

"It complains," I said. "I know which complaint I hear."

Asa lifted a hand for patience. "Keep to the time marks," he said.

Rafi reached for the keyboard and placed a marker at 23:56:00. He typed chime test. He slid to the right. The visual hiss on the waveform stayed even. At 23:59:50 the wall clock ticked loud in the left channel, a clean dry click the desk unit by the rare nook makes when it wakes for the hour. If the phone had sat at Jenna's lap, the clock would live dead center. Left skew meant the mic sat closer to the travel aisle, angled at the endcap, not the circle.

"Eleven fifty-nine fifty," I said into the room. "Clock tick left weighted."

Rafi marked it. Tick loud left.

At 23:59:58 a thin squeak cut the bed. Metal on varnish. Short and sharp. It carried a halo that told me the mic had been within three yards, not eight. That is the difference between being at the endcap and being at Jenna's seat. People think audio is a trick. It is a measuring stick if you respect it.

"Eleven fifty-nine fifty-eight," I said. "Ladder squeak. Close. No voices on top of it."

Rafi marked it and wrote ladder foot squeak, near.

At 00:00:00 the room dropped into a soft noise floor as the bulbs obeyed the hub. The audio bed did not dip, because microphones do not need light to breathe, but the people in the room held breath. Even in a recording you can hear the absence that follows light when it leaves.

Two seconds later, a scrape started. It had the signature of rubber on rug. It did not glide. It hopped. The pattern matched the kink we had chalked by Jenna's chair. The pitch rose as pressure found edge. Then a breath from a woman, pulled in quick through teeth, and a soft word that the mic did not love. It sounded like no. It had the shape of that word in your throat when you do not want to say it loud.

"Zero zero zero three," I said. "Chair drag. Breathy no. Worth a spectral if anyone wants to fight it. But my ear puts the vowel in the right spot."

Rafi marked 00:00:03. Chair drag. Breathy no.

At 00:00:05 the bed lifted by a hair as the bulbs came back. The mic did not care about light. It cared about a chain of bodies snapping from tension to startle. A beat later, at 00:00:06, the thud hit. Heavy on wood. Then the shelf kissed back with a small varnish complaint. The mic took the hit as if it watched. It did not sound like it had watched from a lap six seats away.

"Zero zero zero six," I said. "Thud. Impact on wood. Followed by shelf tap."

Asa nodded. "That lines with the hub log," he said. "Off at the bell. On a handful later. Thud as the light returns."

"Mic sits by the aisle," I said. "Not on her lap. Listen to the HV bed. Listen to the clock. Listen to how the squeak sits in the room."

"Show us," Havel said. He likes to hear proof, not character.

Rafi rolled back to 23:59:40. He tapped a filter to widen the stereo field. He set the room on headphones for Asa and Havel in turn. They took it in. Asa does not pretend to be an engineer. He knows what proximity sounds like. Havel takes notes in scent and sound. He wrote the line. Mic near travel shelf. Squeak at fifty-eight, drag at zero three, thud at zero six.

"Jenna," Asa said. "Your lap did not sit that close to the endcap."

"I moved," she said. "I slid my chair a little before the dip."

"You would have dragged the chair then, not in the dark," I said. "The file hears the scrape at zero three. That is the chair moving during the cut. You said you stood to catch your tote then. You did not say you slid after you stood."

"It is a small room," she said.

"Not that small," Asa said. "Lap audio at your seat would put the clock tick in the center and the fridge pulse under it. I hear neither. I hear the HV branch that lives over the travel shelf and the clock low in the left."

Jenna opened her mouth, closed it, opened it again. "Fine," she said. "I set the phone on the low table near me for better pick up. Still my seat."

"You set it near the lockbox," I said. "You angled it toward the aisle."

She shrugged. "It is ambience," she said. "You want the good sound."

"You want the staged sound," I said. "Good sound takes consent."

Rafi kept playing. At 00:00:10 there was motion on the bed. Shoes. A small scuff. The rubber tone of a tripod foot hitting shelf bottom. A tiny gnat of a squeal. If you live in rooms you learn their noises. If you edit clips you pretend you do not. Jenna stared at her own file like it had betrayed her.

"Tripod touch," I said. "Hello, friend."

"It fell later," she said, reflex firing.

"We will run a reenactment on that," Asa said. "For now we write what the file gives."

Rafi zoomed. At 00:00:03 the chair drag stretched two long syllables the way a rubber foot makes it. At the end of the second, a small breath hit the mic dense. That breath did not live across a ring. It sat close. He marked it. Breathy exhale near mic.

"Move back to fifty," Asa said. "Play me the lead-up."

We rode from 23:59:40 to the bell. A soft rustle at 23:59:55

joined the bed. Not chair. Tote canvas on denim. Zipper tooth on nail. The sound sat at a shallow distance from the capsule. Jenna watched the marker approach that line and gripped her wicker tote like it might turn into a witness.

"There," I said. "Zipper touch five seconds to midnight. Mic two feet away. Not six."

"I checked my bag," she said.

He let the file run. The chime pinged at the back as the bulbs cut. The room took that breath. The chair went. The word came. The thud hit. Everything after that was people being quiet and then being formal.

Rafi stopped the file and saved a copy to a working folder with the tag copy_for_analysis_do_not_modify. He made a second copy and scrubbed silence to destination markers. He named them by time. He printed a one-page shot list of markers with time, label, and notes. He is a dream when a night tries to ask you to get sloppy.

Asa tapped the table with the end of his pen. "Jenna," he said. "State again where the phone sat."

"In my lap," she said. Then she saw her own mistake and pivoted. "On the table by my knees at some points."

"Which," he said.

"Both."

"No," he said. "You moved it for effect. Then you forgot that audio tells the truth. Your file puts your mic near the travel shelf at fifty-eight. It records a zipper within two feet. It hears the clock left. It hears the HVAC branch that lives above that aisle and not the fridge."

She tried one more angle. "I did not stage anything," she said. "I record sound for living memory. People will want to hear what this room felt like."

"This room did not give consent to be turned into content," I said. "You promised ambience. You got chaos and you kept recording."

Her eyes filled with frustration, which looks like tears if you are not paying attention. She was not crying. She was angry that her file loved me more than it loved her. That is where audio always lands. It knows no one.

Rafi pulled the file's metadata and put it on the screen. Creation 23:44:12. Location tag set to Peppermint Cat. Audio format Apple Lossless. No trims logged. He printed that pane. He laid it under the screenshot of the markers. He wrote the hash again on the page in ink.

"Now match to the hub log," Asa said.

Rafi set the Hue print beside the markers. OFF at 00:00:00. ON at 00:00:05. Chair drag at 00:00:03 sat in the dark. Thud at 00:00:06 hit as our bulbs recovered. It fits the stereo memory my body had stored as complaint.

"Run the ten second window over and over," Asa said.

We did. Ladder squeak at fifty-eight. Dip at the bell. Scrape and breath at three. Lift at five. Thud at six. The bed made a pattern and the pattern made a sentence. If you do not respect sentences you should not write anything down.

Havel stepped back with the paper and looked at his small map of the circle from earlier. He drew one more arrow. Mic here. He drew one more small circle. Zipper here at five seconds to midnight. He wrote one more word. Staged.

Jenna saw the word and flinched. "That is not fair," she said. "I told you I do ambience."

"You also told the file manager to hide your location on export," Rafi said. He had not said that out loud yet. He showed us the share dialog, and the option flagged on the last export to compress and strip metadata. "You like control."

"I like clean files," she said. "People do not need to know where I stand for sound."

"Tonight we do," Asa said. "Where you stand matters."

She set her jaw. "You have the raw," she said. "You have your little noises and your vent hum. So what. It is not illegal to record a room."

"It is when you lie about what the file puts where," I said. "We are not court yet. We are chain. This is enough."

Rafi slid the headphones back to me. "One more listen," he said.

I took the ten-second window again and let it live in my head without numbers. It had the shape of a night that got greedy. Squeak. Cut. Scrape. No. Light. Thud. You do not need graduate school to get that line right.

He opened a spectral view and painted the sound into colors for people who cannot hear as hard as they want. The squeak lived high. The scrape sat in the mid. The thud spread like a stain. The clock tick made a neat pin. The HVAC hiss had a wash at 120. The fridge would ring at 90 with a pulsing harmonic. We saw no pulse. We saw the 120 bed and a small peak at 60 when the bulbs came back.

"Good picture," Havel said. He is not impressed by technology. He is impressed by clean work that he can show to a jury without a lecture.

Asa wrote one line and did not raise the pen again until he was done. Audio places mic near travel shelf. Squeak at fifty-eight. Drag and breath at zero three in dark. Thud at zero six as light returns. Subject lied about location. He set the pen down, closed the book, and looked at Jenna the same way he looks at a cheap clock that still keeps good time.

"Where did you put your phone," he said. He did not blink.

"On the table near my seat," she said. "At some point. Toward the aisle. So it would catch the chime."

"Which sits in the back hall," I said. "Not at the endcap."

She ran out of alleyways. She took a breath and gave it to us half straight. "By the travel shelf," she said, low. "I propped it on the map stand at eleven fifty-five."

"Thank you," Asa said. He did not write the thank you. He does not reward late honesty on paper.

Peppermint hopped to the table, sniffed the headphone cable, and batted it twice with a clean paw, then looked away as if embarrassed to share space with audio. He sat, loafed, and blinked. Texture only. He keeps the tone.

Rafi exported the ten-second clip as a stand-alone for the folder. He filed it under PCT_0414_JR_clip_235958_to_000006.wav. He wrote the hash of the clip and stapled it to the print of the markers.

"Next we do placement reenactment," Asa said. "We put a phone where she says she put it. We run the chime. We check levels. Not tonight. Tomorrow. For now we have enough to hold this piece."

Jenna stared at the table. She had built a life on cutting the hunt into digestible bites with music under them. The room had decided to dislike digestion. She swallowed nothing.

"We done," she said, brittle.

"For the audio," Asa said. "Now we look at your gear."

"I brought no rig," she said.

"Your tote says tripod foot," I said. "It left a smudge on the lower shelf that looks like the mark on the rig in your last video. You know the one."

She closed her eyes and let out a breath that read like surrender and tasted like strategy. She would try a new version in five minutes. People do.

Rafi unrolled the chain card for the pod tape and had me initial at the time lines. Havel signed the bottom as witness. Asa put the mirror drive in his case. He does not take more than one copy when the night is raw. He takes what he can protect with his hands.

We stepped back into the main floor. The circle waited. The aisle held. Conrad did not look at the endcap. He watched the door. Margo watched the table where the ballots had been and made a plan to say the sound made her do it.

Asa kept his eyes on Jenna. "You said lap," he said. "Then table. Then aisle. That shift matters."

"It matters to your story," she said.

"It matters to the body," he said.

I looked at the lockbox and at the map stand that waits by the travel shelf with its public maps of old ferry routes and new bus lines. A small smear on its edge glinted. Oil from a thumb had met dust. I put a scale card there and took a quick photo. It would pay later. Not a smoking anything. A placement.

"Time zero fifty-eight," I said. "Audio markers logged. Mic placement near travel shelf noted. Subject revised her claim. We proceed to gear."

Jenna tucked her phone into her tote with a soft scrape as if hiding shame were a sound she could call her own. Asa let the lie sit in the open air. He likes to let people drown their own words. He wrote a short note. Then he folded the book and pocketed his pen.

End of lesson.

CHAPTER 9

Card in Jacket

The used cart sat where it always sits on club nights. End of the counter. One wheel that squeaks when it wants attention. Jackets stacked spine up in tidy rows for Monday pricing. Peppermint hopped onto the corner and settled into a loaf that said he owned the inventory and the air.

"Two minutes," Asa said. "Then we go back to the aisle."

"Enough," I said. "This will not take long."

I pulled the first handful of jackets to the flat of the cart. Cloth over board. Midlist hardbacks from eight years ago that die slow and earn their keep with one clean sale. One jacket wore a gloss sleeve we had not put on it. Library mylar. Tight tape lines, brittle at the fold. A faint ghost rectangle on the back where a pocket once lived. Old glue shadow. I slid a scale card under the flap and lifted the fore-edge fold with a gloved fingernail.

Something resisted. Not tape. A slip tucked deep. I eased it out with the card as a blade.

A card. Cream, worn thin, corners rounded by years in a pocket. Ashmead County Public Library across the top in a serif that liked to be noticed. Below, stamped lines. Name: Benji Hsu. Borrower number. A barcode applied crooked fifteen years ago or by a clerk in a hurry. The last date stamp sat bold and blue by a hand that smacked paper for a living. 2017 APR 02. The ink had bled into the fibers a hair and then gone to sleep. Nothing fresh. No wet. No new.

Peppermint leaned forward to sniff and then blinked, offended by dry card smell. He looked at Benji as if to ask him to read his own past.

"Bring him," Asa said.

Benji stood three yards away and had been pretending not to watch us handle a stack. He came when I nodded, hands visible, jacket still buttoned though the room had warmed. He kept the distance a man keeps when he knows his name is on the object.

"What am I seeing," he asked. Calm voice. Eyes on the card.

I tipped the card so he could read the lines. "Ashmead County," I said. "Borrower name. Yours."

His face flushed from collar to ear in one wash. He had the decency not to pretend to be surprised past the first breath. He nodded once like a person who sees an old bruise in a mirror.

"That is mine," he said. "From before I moved here."

"Under a jacket flap," Asa said. "On my cart, tonight."

"It must have ridden in," he said. "I had an extra stack of jackets in my trunk when I came by last week for the Thursday swap. I brought them in. I did not check every flap."

"Origin of the jackets," I said.

"Donations shelf at the Ashmead Friends sale," he said. "After a split with the club there. I left in a hurry. I took the jackets I had contributed and a few orphans from the discard table. I told myself I would make amends later with a check. I have the email. You can pull it."

"Split," Havel said. Not an accusation. A word on a shelf.

"Loud," Benji said. "Stupid. Not violent. People picked teams and called each other names about curation and access. I walked. I could not sit in a room where hypocrisy passed for taste. That was two years ago. The jacket pile moved with me. I forgot it behind a box of pots. Found it last week. Brought it in to ask Liora if she could use the sleeves or the art for a wall. I set the stack on this cart while we talked about the kid program. I never looked under the flaps."

I turned the card and looked at the stamp again. 2017 APR 02. Not last week. Not last month. Old. It lived where history belongs.

"Chain," I said.

Rafi had the tray ready before I asked. He slid the glassine across the counter. I set the card in, printed the label, and wrote the quick line. Ashmead County PL borrower card, name Benji Hsu, found under fore-edge flap of used hardback jacket on shop cart, time 01:06. I signed across the tape and passed the sleeve to Asa. He signed under me and set it on the lockbox table like an object that knew its place.

I lifted the jacket and laid it flat. The spine worn, publisher logo stamped in white, the crease at the flap edge cracked where fingers had lived. The mylar had yellowed at the fold. Library tape shining, split at one corner. On the back panel a rectangular glue shadow darker than the surrounding paper. A pocket once sat there. Gone now. The outline looked like a ghost bed.

"Photograph," I said.

Rafi set the scale card by the flap, placed today's paper in frame, and shot top, side, and detail on the pocket shadow. He shot the glue ridges under raking light. He shot the mylar's yellowing at the fold, which speaks in the way paper speaks when it has seen a decade and some cleaning fluid.

"What book," Havel said.

I flipped the spine. A midlist thriller that will not break a heart. The sort of thing you buy two for the shop during tourist season and watch them leave by August. The jacket art looked tired. The barcode on the outside had been peeled long ago. A whisper of adhesive still lived there. The book inside had already been sold last winter to a customer who wanted the text block for a class.

We keep jackets when the art sells better than the spine.

"This jacket sat in my back room for a week," I said. "We had not priced it. It did not belong to tonight. The card did not walk under its own power."

Benji nodded. "It rode under the flap when I packed the jackets two years ago," he said. "The pockets at Ashmead still had old cards in them for the Friends sale. Volunteers pulled some. Not all. People took home jackets for art. We tucked flaps and forgot. I packed mine. It would be stupid to pretend I do not know that look."

"Date stamp," Asa said.

"Old," I said. "2017. Ink bled and dried. Face of the card touched mylar for years. You can see the gloss transfer at the corner where it lived pressed."

Rafi shot a close-up of the stamp with the scale. He set the photo next to the sleeve. Havel wrote old in his book and underlined it once. He does not indulge in leaps when two steps suffice.

"Red herring," he said, quiet.

"History," I said. "A thing that belongs to his past that found a rude way to be present."

Benji watched my face the way people watch a judge. "You want me to say the rest," he said.

"If it keeps us from guessing," I said.

"I left Ashmead because the club there turned into a show," he said. "A podcaster got traction on a stupid segment about shaming paperbacks. The moderator leaned into it. I spoke against it. They called me humorless and old-school. Then someone shoved a student at an open mic who asked about access. I did not wait for a vote. I wrote an email to the branch manager and I walked home. I did not punch anyone. I did not push anyone down a ladder. I did not bring a stunt to your floor."

Asa looked at his notes. "You did not fight with Erica here," he said.

Benji shook his head. "I hardly knew her," he said. "We exchanged two notes about a bus route in a book and an author whose archive lives at my old library. She liked clean scan dates. So do I. That is all."

"Witness," I said.

"Me," Rafi said. "He came in last week with jackets at three in the afternoon. He left them here and went to the back to ask Liora about a kid shelf idea. He did not circle the counter. He did not touch the lockbox table. He did not sit in every chair to see which one squeaks. He is not that bored."

Peppermint stretched and put one paw on the cart wheel to stop its complaint. He blinked at Benji and approved of none of this. That is his brand.

I slid the jacket into a sleeve big enough for picture books and wrote the line on the card. Used hardback jacket with library mylar and pocket shadow. Card found under fore-edge flap. Bagged with card sleeve. I signed and taped it clean. Asa signed. Havel initialed. We do not make a fuss with cardboard and tape. We still do it.

"Where did you keep your jackets in your trunk," Asa said to Benji. "Bag. Box. Loose."

"In a banker's box," he said. "Two rolls of tape, a handful of old jackets I never got around to listing, a velvet rope from a display I never wanted to use. The card must have settled inside one flap in that mess. Or I tucked it there in 2017 when I did not have my wallet. I do not remember. That was a season I try not to invite back."

"Email to the branch manager," Havel said.

"I can forward it," Benji said. "I wrote it from my personal account. It has the date. It also has language I wish I had phrased with less acid."

"Send it when the room is calm," Asa said. "Tonight we note that the past wants to dress up as the present. We decline the costume."

Conrad drifted closer, uninvited, as if the cart were a podium. He looked at the card and then at Benji and tried a tone that sounds like leadership if you are tired. "Background matters," he said. "People repeat patterns."

"People also learn," I said. "The card is old. The stamp is older. The Ashmead story belongs to him and to a room that is not mine. We will not let it pay rent here."

He smiled without warmth. It did not help him.

Jenna hovered at a safe distance and took in the card with bright eyes that see content and not consequence. "It is a good beat for a segment," she said. "Past lives in the flaps of our present. A metaphor."

"Save it for your feed," I said. "Do not repurpose my floor."

She raised both hands in a show of surrender that fooled no one and backed off a single step.

I turned the jacket over again and looked at the inside back flap. A tiny pencil number sat near the price box. 3.00. Friends sale. Someone wrote it at a folding table in a gym that smells like dust and old oranges. The graphite had polished under the mylar and sat dull and honest. I photographed it. More chain for a story I hope we never have to tell out loud.

Havel took the sleeve with the card and weighed it in his palm like an apple. "You should still log it," he said to me, though I had already done it. "History tends to return with new shoes."

"It stays here," I said. "If Ashmead calls, they will get an apology and a donation from me and a note that their pocket policy needs a second glance."

Benji exhaled. The color left his face and returned in a pattern that made sense. Shame is a bad map. It draws detours where you do not need them.

"Do you believe me," he said. He did not plead for it. He asked as a man who has built a life on the side of a line and prefers it that way.

"I believe you left a room when it asked you to choose cruelty," I said. "I believe your name sits on a card from 2017 and not on my floor at midnight. I believe the jacket rode here because our lives are messy and our trunks are small."

He nodded. "Thank you," he said. "For not turning that into a script."

"Do not thank me yet," I said. "You still owe me an inventory hour on Tuesday for bringing me mystery without consent."

"Done," he said. He looked relieved to pay with work.

Asa closed the sleeve and set it in the evidence stack on the table with a clean barrier between it and the ballots. He likes to keep stories from touching if they do not have to. I like that too.

Rafi wrote one more line on the counter log. Jacket card found and bagged, time 01:12. He drew a small cat in the corner because Peppermint had kept a paw on the cart while we worked and that amuses him when the night refuses to.

I paged the shop phone camera and took a final wide shot for the binder. Cart, jacket sleeve, card sleeve, scale card, today's paper. I spoke the time without raising my voice.

"Time zero one thirteen," I said. "Ashmead County card logged. Stamp date old. Jacket bagged. This points to history, not tonight."

Benji looked at the aisle and then back at the cart. "I never fought with Erica," he said. "I liked her spine. She did not waste people's time. If I had said something wrong, she would have told me in two words and I would have said thanks."

"That is the kind of fight she had," I said. "If only."

He nodded again and went back to his chair, smaller than when he walked up and in a better way. Sometimes the act of telling the truth gives a person permission to sit like himself.

Peppermint hopped off the cart and head-butted my knee. He does not love chain. He respects it. He went to the counter and chirped at the empty space where the kettle should be. Miss

Dotty would have had tea by now. Tonight the kettle waited for when the city let us breathe.

Havel glanced toward the aisle and then to Asa. "Back to the path," he said.

"As planned," Asa said. He picked up the sleeves and his notebook. He watched Benji sit. He watched Conrad watch the door. He watched Margo straighten the edges of her tote with tiny hungry movements, as if order might let her out of the box she built for herself.

I slid the jacket sleeve into the case file and set a divider between it and the ballots. I wrote a small sticker for the spine. Red herring. Old. It keeps me honest later when somebody tries to dramatize.

Benji raised a palm. "You want the club email now," he said.

"Tomorrow," I said. "Send it after you sleep and before you overthink. Use a subject line I can search for when my head aches."

He smiled with a corner of his mouth. "Subject line, I walked away," he said.

"Good," I said. "The city could use more of those."

We moved as a group back toward the aisle and the chalk line and the bell. Rafi pushed the cart an inch so the wheel would not complain, then set a small wedge under it with his shoe. Peppermint approved of the silence and trotted ahead like a small usher.

I looked once more at the old card in its sleeve. It looked harmless. That is the trick with paper. It carries harm and help the same way. You have to read the stamp and the glue and the way a corner feels when it has known a pocket longer than it should.

"Chain is chain," Asa said, catching my look. "Even when it points backward."

"Especially then," I said.

We stepped into the circle's edge. The rug held the chalk. The table held the prints. The lockbox held the sleeping phones. The timer phone kept its small green circle like a toy that wanted to be a tool and never would be again.

"Log the last line," Asa said.

I did. "Benji denies any fight with Erica," I said for the room and the page. "I log the jacket chain anyway."

CHAPTER 10

Ladder Foot

The back room keeps our small religion. Shelves in rows. Labels straight. Notes that tell the future where to stand.

Rafi flicked the chain on the pull light. "Supplies shelf," he said. "Left bay."

I set the ladder on a moving blanket in the center so we would not smear what we needed. The left foot with the gray bloom faced me. The right foot sat clean. I could smell citrus before I reached the bottles.

"Yesterday we waxed only the travel aisle," Rafi said. "I logged it."

He pulled the clipboard from the hook. The sheet read Floor plan work, 04.14, 17:05 to 17:45. Travel aisle only, citrus polymer, thin coat, buff by hand, cones up until close. His initials sat tight along the margin. He had underlined travel. Miss Dotty likes that underline. I do too.

I set the clipboard by the ladder. "Chain reads," I said. "We did one strip. Scent matches the aisle."

I took the bottle down. Clear plastic. White cap. Orange label with a list of things a sales rep loves and I ignore. The liquid inside shone pale with a slight haze. I cracked the cap and let the room have it. Citrus walked out and put a hand on our throats. Not sweet. Solvent. It smelled like a peel you forgot on a radiator.

I glanced at Asa. He tilted the bottle and nodded.

"Citrus base," he said. "Your scrape said the same."

Rafi brought the open pack of peel pads. Twelve to a sheet when you buy them new. Our pack had five left on the backing and one missing space on the second strip where a pad had been pulled. The torn edge showed yesterday's haste.

"Count," he said.

I counted with a gloved finger. "Eleven used," I said. "Five left. One empty square. You open this at 17:12," I added, reading his note on the bag in his small block hand.

"Receipt is in the till," he said. "We bought that pack at 5:12 p.m. when I realized the old feet were past their patience."

"Good," Asa said. He looked at the ladder feet again. "One side shows transfer. One side clean. That clean sits on the side that would lift if you swing the ladder instead of set it."

I crouched. The left pad showed the gray chalk bloom we saw on the floor. Under it a faint trace of orange lit at the edge when I angled the light. Wax takes on the bottle's tint when it dries thin, a cheat for the impatient eye. The right pad held no bloom. The rubber showed a soft wear haze from its months of life and nothing for tonight.

"Photograph," I said.

Rafi set the scale card against the left pad and took one wide and one close. He turned the ladder half a hand and shot the right pad with the same frame. I read the time.

"Time zero one twenty," I said. "Left foot carries gray scuff with citrus odor and faint orange cast. Right foot clean. Matches a swing, not a set."

We pulled a clean white tag card from the drawer. I touched the edge of the gray bloom with the tag and picked up a thin dust from the pad. It tinted the paper a breath darker. I held the card over the bottle mouth and let the vapor pass. It woke the scent again. Citrus. Not floor dirt. I put that card in a glassine and wrote one line. Transfer dust from ladder left foot. Citrus odor when warmed. I signed. Asa signed. Rafi sealed it.

Havel stepped closer and took the bottle from my hand. "You used this on the travel aisle," he said. "Only there."

"Only," Rafi said. "We put cones and a bar down for an hour. Liora kept the circle away. No one walked the strip except me while I buffed."

"Your shoes," Havel said.

Rafi showed his soles. I checked for any residue that would tell a bad story. Clean. He had kept to the paper squares he lays down when he does the job he loves. Habit beats drama.

I set a fresh peel pad next to the left foot to match sizes. The diameters spoke together. I did not press it on. I wanted the camera to see before we stuck anything anywhere.

"The missing pad from the pack could be our future," I said. "If we find it stuck to a foot, we close a loop between this shelf and the aisle."

"Later," Asa said. "For now we prove this scrape is ours."

Rafi reached up for the small fan from the top shelf and clicked it on low. Solvent can fog a head if you live with it. I let the air move while I did the next small ugly job.

"Swab," I said.

He handed me two cottons and a vial. I touched one swab to the left pad where the gray sat thickest and rolled it once to pick up dust and oil. I did the same on the right pad for a control. I labeled both. Ladder left, ladder right. I capped the vial around the pair and taped the seam. If a lab ever needed to hear from me, it would not have to guess what I sent.

"Bottle, card," Asa said.

I tipped a drop of the wax on a test card. It flashed clear, then set with that same faint amber sigh. I brought the left pad near the card without pressing and looked at the shades under the back room light. Twins. The lab will love this more than it deserves. I loved it enough.

"Photograph," I said.

Rafi shot the bottle, the test card, and the foot in the same frame with the scale. He shot the pad count on the open pack with the torn slot to show one missing. He shot the clipboard log that read travel aisle only. He shot his own initials because it keeps the form clean when a person says the clerk staged a shelf.

"Yesterday you buffed by hand," Asa said.

"I did," Rafi said. "Clean rag. Straight lines. I can show you the strokes if you kneel by the endcap. The grain carries them. That is how we knew the ladder foot did not set. It skidded across my stitch."

"Match it," Asa said.

I brought the ladder foot pad to the test card that held the drop we had set. I touched one edge of the pad to the edge of the card and let them kiss. When I lifted away, the card kept a faint dark arc like a tiny quarter moon. That shape matched the curve the pad had left on the travel aisle floor under the endcap. I did not need to say it. Havel nodded.

"Color," he said. "Scent. Shape. Local."

"Local," I said again. "Nothing on the rest of the shop wears this. We did not do the rare nook. We did not do the children's bay. We did only the travel aisle for this week because the tour group tracks dust where they stand to argue over hostels."

Rafi grinned without humor. He knows that group. We all do.

Asa squatted and sighted along the ladder rung. "If a person stands at Jenna's chair and grabs the ladder midpoint, then swings it in a hurry to clear a path or to stage a pose, the right foot lifts. The left drags first. The first contact will be left pad to fresh wax. That gives us the gray scuff."

"Swing," I said. "Not set."

"Swing," he said.

I looked at the back room floor and saw what my body had

sketched while I stood in the aisle earlier. You do a thing a hundred times and your muscles learn to write that verb. Swing. I had swung ladders into line in my life. You can feel the moment where one foot stops talking to the floor.

"Take the ladder back in," Havel said. "I want one detail for my book, then we bag."

"Before we move," I said, "we log the pad pack and the bottle for the record."

We did. I wrote two cards. Citrus floor finish, one bottle, opened 04.14 at 17:05, used only on travel aisle per log. Peel pad pack, missing one space on strip two, five pads left, opened 17:12. I signed, Rafi signed, Asa initialed. We bagged both in clear sleeves and set them on the shelf with a quiet that felt like dignity for plastic.

Rafi brought a small trash sack from under the sink. He always has one ready for fibers. He sealed the top with a twist, then wrote the simple line on a label. Ladder area sweepings, pre-bag. He would walk the blanket after we moved the ladder to catch any crumbs we dislodged. The best time to be fussy is now, not when a person points at a photo and calls you sloppy.

We lifted the ladder together by the side rails so we would not smear the foot. We took it like a stretcher, steady and level, back to the aisle. The cones on the travel strip still sat against the endcaps from last night's cure. I set them back as if the cones were markers in a field.

"Hold," Asa said.

He kneelt at the threshold and looked at the grain. He does not love floors. He respects them. He set the left foot in the air a finger above the strip. He did not let it touch.

"Smell tells me here," he said. "Eye tells me this foot kissed this strip and jumped."

"And right foot," I said.

"Lifted," he said. "Which means a person guided the ladder from the right, not the left. That puts them closer to Jenna's seat than to Erica's."

"Which fits the scrape," I said. "And the way the chair turned. Arm reached in from Jenna's vector, grabbed the rung, pulled, pivoted, and let the thing go."

"Let or lost," Havel said.

"Lost works too," I said. "I will take either if the rest of the room agrees."

We set the ladder down, careful, on the moving blanket again. The left pad looked smug. It should not have. No object should ever look pleased with its own role in a night like this.

"Bag it," Asa said.

Rafi slid the long sleeve over the ladder and pulled the zip across the top. He taped the seal. He wrote Ladder, travel aisle, left foot scrape, bagged 01:34, and passed me the pen. I signed across the tape. Asa signed under. Havel initialed the corner. He likes corners. Corners hide nothing.

"Blackout test," Asa said next, as if he were ordering tea. "We run a two-second dip and a five-second return. We place people where they sat. We do not let anyone perform. We will watch the chair vector and listen for the scrape. We will log when the ladder wants to move even when no hand touches it, and then when a hand does."

"Tonight," I said.

"In an hour," he said. "When the coroner clears and I can put people in the room without disrespect."

He looked at Margo, then at Jenna. "You will stand where you sat," he said. "You will keep your hands visible. You will not touch a thing without me telling you to. If a phone vibrates, you will let it. If a thought vibrates, you will keep it to yourself."

They did not argue. Even their faces decided now was not the time.

Rafi took the bottle and the pad pack back to the shelf for now. He set the cards where the camera could see if anyone asked later. He straightened the missing pad slot again, then clicked the bag closed with more care than plastic deserves. He can make a ritual out of cheap things and dignify them. I try and do not always win. He wins.

I pulled one more test. A control pad that had never met a floor. I pressed it to the test card next to the bottle's drop. Clean edge. No cast. No solvent perfume on heat. I labeled it Control. I slipped it into the glassine with the dust card and wrote control on the flap with a small arrow for the lab to ignore or love. Either is fine.

"Statement," Havel said.

I gave it to him like a teacher friendly with grades. "Yesterday we waxed only the travel aisle with a citrus polymer. The ladder's left foot shows a fresh gray scrape with citrus odor and a faint orange cast that matches the bottle on our shelf. The right foot is clean. That says swing, not set. The peel pad pack we opened at 17:12 shows one pad missing from its strip. We have not found that pad yet. We will."

He wrote it. Each word. He does not quote when he can write a clean paraphrase. He did not need to this time. He liked my line.

"Time," Asa said.

"Zero one thirty-six," I said. "Ladder foot matched to the travel aisle wax by color and scent. Left foot shows transfer. Right foot lifted during a swing. Peel pad pack missing one pad. Bottle and pack logged. Ladder bagged. Asa schedules a blackout test."

Peppermint appeared at the end of the aisle like he had been napping in the only pure spot left in the city. He sprung to the top shelf and looked down at the bagged ladder with disdain. He blinked at the cones. He gave me one small chatty chirp, the kind that says I prefer dignity and I will accept none of this.

"Noted," I said to him. "We will get your dignity back on the shelf by noon."

He yawned like a lion and settled into a loaf that suggested the ladder could think about its choices. He is not a solver. He reminds the room what it should be when we are done.

Asa tapped the bag once with the back of his hand. "This thing will not move again until we ask it to," he said. "When we dim the room and let the chair tell us its story, we will be ready for the way people lie about their arms."

"People always do," I said.

We moved back to the counter to stage the rest. The Hue log waited. The router print waited. The ballots in sleeves waited. The jacket card slept in its evidence pouch like a ghost satisfied to be documented. The shop clock carried us toward the test. The street had given up trying to tell us what to do. Good. We had a plan.

I wrote one last card for the binder so the morning crew would not step into a mess without context. Ladder bagged. Do not touch. Travel aisle closed for test. Blackout run scheduled. Then I tore a piece of blue tape and stuck it along the edge of the aisle with two words in block letters. No entry.

Peppermint approved. He jumped down, walked along the tape like a parade marshal, and sat by the lockbox as if it were a throne. He thumped his tail once. Verdict delivered.

Asa looked at the room and then at me. "Ready," he said.

"As I will be," I said.

We had done what a room asks of you when it bleeds. Document. Separate. Match. Keep faith with the floor. Then make people stand where they stood and ask the night to show its hands.

CHAPTER 11

Gran Remembers

Gran's garage smells like oil, cedar, and paper that earned its keep. Pegboard on three walls. Labeled bins. A workbench that has seen every school project in this family since before I learned the alphabet. She keeps a ledger on a slanted stand. It is a clothbound book with a spine so honest it squeaks.

"Door up or down," Gran said.

"Up," I said. "Good light helps a lie keep its distance."

She pushed the door. Morning gray came in and made the dust polite. Peppermint rode over in his carrier because he insists. I set him on the bench and unclipped the latch. He stepped out, sniffed a jar of screws, and chose the ledge near the ledger like a clerk who does not clock in.

"We have a ream to find," I said. "Cat's-eye. Donation stock. Last summer."

Gran opened the ledger where the ribbon sat. She did not check an index. She knew the page. She tapped a line with her fingernail and tilted the book toward me.

Entry reads:

CAT'S-EYE REAM. 500 sheets. Watermark test cut OK. Received 06.12. Used for Blind Date Night 08.14. Balance after event: 0.

Notes: leftovers signed out post-cleanup by M. Ellsworth. See volunteer slip.

Her pencil tick lived next to the zero. She puts one by every item that reaches its end. Her ticks are tidy. They carry judgment.

"You told me we ran it out," I said.

"We did," she said. "Here."

She flipped two pages back to a small pocket taped into the gutter. Inside lay a half sheet of yellow paper with a carbon copy beneath.

Volunteer slip, materials removal after event.
Date 08.14. Time 22:50.
Name: Margo Ellsworth.
Item: Cat's-eye ream leftovers, approximately one dozen sheets, remainder of cut stack and display scraps.
Purpose: community club signage.
Approved: G. Wren.
Signature: M. Ellsworth.

Gran's signature sat neat in blue pen. Margo's sat tight in black. The time placed her here after the last table was wiped and the last blind-date wrap was stacked for the recycler.

"She asked for scraps," Gran said. "Not a crime. I sign for every removal. She smiled and said the club would use scraps for bookmarks or quote cards. Her tote was clean. She stood by the back door, not the counter. I do not love that posture."

"Did she take full sheets," I said.

"She took what was left on the cut board," Gran said. "Not many. The ream wrapper went into the bin. The ledger went to zero. The shop had nothing left. That is what I told you on the phone."

"That matches," I said. "We found ballots on cat's-eye stock. We found a copier ring on every sheet. The bottom blank from the stack downstairs carries that ring. The watermark sits in the same place as your test cut."

Gran reached to the shelf above the bench and pulled down

a clear envelope. Inside sat the ream wrapper with a stapled sample square. She keeps one square from every special stock, labeled, drilled for a binder that exists only in her mind.

She laid the sample against the light. The cat's-eye winked in the fibers. Two ovals. One slit. The slit sat right of center on the lower half. I held a ballot from my bag to the light beside it. The mark nested.

"Same placement," Gran said. "Same press. The wrap tells the mill. I kept it because I like to win arguments."

She let that sit. It warmed the room.

"Photograph," I said.

I set today's paper in frame, placed the scale card by the ledger line, shot the entry, the volunteer slip, and the wrapper with the sample. I read the time for the room. Gran likes form when the world goes sideways.

"Time nine oh seven," I said. "Ledger shows cat's-eye ream used for Blind Date Night 08.14. Balance zero. Volunteer slip shows leftovers signed out by M. Ellsworth at 22:50 for club signage. Wrapper with sample retained."

Gran returned the wrapper to its envelope and slid it back to its slot. She turned and pointed with her whole hand, the way she does when a lesson wants to land.

"Leftovers live here until I say otherwise," she said. "People put away scraps like they put away guilt. I do not let either clutter my house."

She crossed to a plastic bin labeled OFFCUTS, EVENT. She popped the lid. Inside sat the history of shop nights in curls and squares. Kraft strips from wrap stations. Marbled endsheet corners from a donations sort. A small rubber-banded packet of cat's-eye trimmings, eight pieces no bigger than a palm.

"Margo did not take these," she said. "These are my offcuts. The slip covers the rest that sat on the cut table after we measured jackets. She asked at the end. She said, do you mind if the club uses the remainder for cards. I said sign here. I will sleep fine.

That was before she found the word procedure and tried to marry it."

"You signed her out at 22:50," I said. "We have her PDF on our queue at 10:02 p.m. tonight. Same header as her chat graphic. She had marked stock in her closet since August."

"Margo keeps leftovers," Gran said.

The sentence sat on the bench like a weight. Peppermint flicked an ear as if he heard the click. He put his chin on the ledger and closed his eyes. Texture, not help. Still true.

I slid the volunteer slip into a sleeve and filled a card. Volunteer removal slip, 08.14, M. Ellsworth, cat's-eye leftovers, signed by G. Wren. Photographed with ledger and wrapper. I signed the tape and handed it to Gran to initial. She did. Her initials are the opposite of fancy.

"What about the chamber copier," she said. "You mentioned a ring."

"The bottom blank from the ballot stack carries a faint coffee ring ghost," I said. "Same nick in the circle repeats on the filled ballots. Our copier glass is clean. The chamber glass is not. We will photograph their platen today and print a test blank to match the nick. Then we lay it over our bottom sheet. It will marry."

Gran nodded. "You will be polite to the clerk," she said. "She is tired of men who lean on her counter and call a smudge a personal attack. She pours a lot of coffee and has no patience for cups on glass. Bring her a lint-free cloth and a kind word. She will open the lid for you."

"I will," I said.

Gran flipped two more pages in the ledger and tapped another line, because she refuses to let one fact carry alone when a second can reinforce it.

BLIND DATE NIGHT WRAP COUNT. Cat's-eye used: 482 sheets. Offcuts returned to OFFCUTS bin. Leftover whole sheets signed out to M. Ellsworth. Scrap remainder in OFFCUTS bin, eight pieces. Balance zero.

She had totaled the numbers with the implacable mercy of a math teacher. It left no room for the word stash. We did not keep anything on site that could feed secret ballots. If ballots lived, they lived because a person walked them out.

"Do you need the board signature," she said.

"I need your memory," I said. "And your sign-out slip. The board will want your neat lines if a lawyer decides to chew."

"They always do," she said. "It is why God made pencils."

She reached under the bench and brought up a cigar box she uses for the shop's petty stamps and for the three coins that belong to the loose change story she tells children when they refuse to give back a marble. From the box she lifted a small ink pad and the stamp that lives in the ledger margin. She stamped the volunteer slip's corner with the cat's-eye she drew by hand forty years ago. She smiled. She likes when a symbol finds its way home.

"Bring this back," she said. "I do not make second stamps to flatter a court."

"I will bring it back," I said. "We are doing this right."

"You are a clerk," she said. "Do not let anyone call you anything else. The world gets sloppy when clerks forget who they are."

She pulled a torn page from a steno pad and wrote a line for me to slide into the shop case file as a summary in her hand.

Cat's-eye ream: all used at Blind Date Night 08.14. Shop retained only offcuts. Whole-sheet leftovers signed out by M. Ellsworth, 22:50, for club. No remaining inventory at Peppermint Cat after that date. G.W.

She signed the bottom as if it were a check and handed it to me. I slid it into a sleeve and taped it. I took one more photograph with the ledger, the stamp, and the wrapper. Today's paper in the corner. Time on my phone in the frame.

"Time nine fourteen," I said. "Ledger and volunteer slip establish cat's-eye exit to Margo. Wrapper sample confirms mark placement. Offcuts present, tiny. Whole sheets gone since August."

Gran wiped a non-existent smudge off the ledger page with the side of her hand. She does that when she thinks about people who try to fog thin air.

"I remember that night," she said. "She stayed late. Smiled with nothing behind it. Said thank you three times and acted like she wanted a stage. I put the scrap bundle in OFFCUTS and made her sign for the rest. She did not love the pen."

"She likes ceremony," I said.

"She likes control dressed as ceremony," Gran said. "Do not let the city pay her for the costume."

I looked around the garage at the order that kept our family honest. Gran had built half of it from scraps. The rest she bought with coupons and sanded until it looked like it wanted to live. She runs this place with ledgers and habit. The shop learned its bones here.

"Any chance another person took cat's-eye after the event," I said. "No slip."

"No," she said. "I stood at the door. People do not pass me with paper unless I like their reasons."

She pulled the OFFCUTS packet of cat's-eye and shook it in my hand. The sound was small and dry. Not enough to feed a ballot army. Enough to underline a line in a ledger if you needed a physical anchor.

"That is what leftovers look like," she said. "What she took were not leftovers in my book. They were the last of the stock. Do not let her spin."

"I will not," I said.

Peppermint leaped to the floor and sat on my shoe like a stamp. He likes to close scenes. He knows when to take a bow without applause.

"Coffee," Gran said.

"In a minute," I said. "I need one last card."

I wrote the card for the binder we keep under the counter. Cat's-eye provenance locked. Ream exhausted 08.14. M. Ellsworth signed out last whole sheets 22:50 for club signage. Shop retains only small offcuts. Wrapper sample preserved. Ledger and slip photographed, bagged, and signed. I dated the card and drew a tiny cat's-eye next to the word locked. Gran peered over and approved my sloppy art with a grunt.

"You will go to the chamber," she said. "You will show the ring. You will make the clerk smile."

"I will," I said.

She closed the ledger with the care of a person who expects to open it again. She set the stamp and pad in their cigar box and slid the box home. She put her hand on the OFFCUTS lid and pushed it down until it clicked.

"People think bins are neutral," she said. "They are not. They tell you what a room believes about time. I believe in closing a cycle. She believes in keeping leftovers. That difference will teach you something every time."

I stood with the sleeve in my hand and let that line tidy itself. It did not need my help. It belonged in the book.

"Say it again," I said.

Gran looked at the ledger and then at me. Her eyes had the same steady temperature they have when a contractor tries to sell her nonsense.

"She keeps leftovers," Gran said.

It landed.

CHAPTER 12

Rafi's Roster

The counter looked ready to testify. Clipboard. Till tape. Pen that writes through grease. Rafi already had the sign-in sheet flat and the espresso drawer open to the 5 p.m. roll.

"Grid first," he said. "Names, times, positions."

"Run it," I said.

He tapped the sheet with his nail. My neat block letters at the top. Midnight Reading Club. Sign in, seat, arrival time.

"Benji Hsu," Rafi read. "Arrived 11:20. Sat left of circle, seat B."

Benji's hand had printed his name like he was filling a card at a library. Clean. He had added a tiny dot over the j in habit, not flourish. I took a photo with the scale card and today's paper in frame. I spoke the minute.

"Time zero nine twenty-eight," I said. "Sign-in for Benji Hsu, 11:20, seat B."

"Jenna Roarke," Rafi read next. "Arrived 11:30. Note says set up near travel shelf."

The note was mine. I do not love that I had written it. I did it because I thought supervision would keep the rig honest. I took another photo.

"Time zero nine twenty-nine," I said. "Sign-in for Jenna Roarke,

11:30, placement near travel shelf."

"Conrad Vale," Rafi said. "Arrived 11:18. Seat C. Marked 'phone out twice.'"

That mark was Rafi's. A small square with two slashes, the way he notes a break in a coffee rush. He circled the block when a person stepped away from a circle. It helps later when stories want to braid themselves.

"Margo Ellsworth," he said. "Arrived 11:12. Seat D. Checked the lockbox three times."

"How do you know three," Asa said.

Rafi lifted a second sheet. "Host tasks," he said. "I jot when folks hover our hardware. She put hands on the table at 23:20, 23:43, and 23:58. No lid lifts. Just inventory glances. I wrote her words too. 'I like to see the hardware. Settles the room.'"

"Photograph both sheets," Asa said.

I did. Scale card. Today's paper. One-wide, one-detail on each entry that was going to matter later.

"The rest," Rafi said, flipping the board. "Erica at 11:10, seat A, moderator. Liora here, of course. Rafi at 17:05 for floor. Peppermint, unhelpful."

Peppermint blinked at that line and put his chin on the card reader as if to garnish it.

"The till," I said.

Rafi printed the late shift tape. He snapped the narrow strip loose and laid it next to the sign-in. He traced the roll with a finger, counting back by time blocks.

"Floor maintenance pack," he read. "SKU FP-12. 17:12, one unit. Citrus polymer, 17:05, one bottle. Buff pads pack, 17:08, one. Charge Rafi, cash drawer reconciling."

I shot the strip with the scale card and wrote a small card for the binder. Purchase times match floor work log. 17:12 peel pad pack. 17:05 citrus polymer. I clipped the card to the strip with a binder clip and laid it by the sign-in.

"We bought the peel pads at 5:12," I said, for the record. "One strip shows a missing space. We have not found the missing pad. Yet."

Rafi nodded. "I opened that pack at 17:12 on the shelf," he said. "I wrote it on the bag. We used eleven to refresh ladders and stools. One spot on the sheet is empty from a pull."

Havel wrote one word. Missing. He underlined it. He looked at the ladder bag in the aisle like it owed him a favor.

"Now the espresso till as clock," Asa said. "Who bought what tells me when a person stood close enough to the counter to speak. That anchors movement."

Rafi scrolled the items. "Double for Benji at 11:21," he said. "Croissant he did not eat. He uses pastry as a napkin weight."

"True," Benji said from the circle, half a smile. He had not moved. His hand sat on his knee the way he puts it when he wants to be counted as steady.

"Jenna's tea at 11:32," Rafi said. "Honey ask. She always says she is fighting a throat tick. She likes a prop."

"Conrad, water at 11:41, returned at 11:53 for another," Rafi said. "Short visits. He took both to the back door for phone calls. I noted back door in my side log because he leaned into the jamb and said 'give me a second' to the alley like it owed him time."

"Mark those," Asa said.

I wrote short cards. Conrad water 11:41. Conrad water 11:53. Back door use for calls. I clipped them to the till strip and took a photo.

"Margo, nothing from the till after 9," Rafi said. "She ate a bar from her tote. She used our napkins for the wrapper. She checked the lockbox and told me to set an extra pen on the table. I set one with a dead cartridge to see who would test it. No one did. She brought her own."

"Three lockbox checks," Asa said again, because repetition crodes a defense. "Times."

"Twenty past, forty-three, fifty-eight," Rafi said. "At fifty-eight she stood, looked at the box, looked at the circle, and adjusted her blazer like ceremony had arrived."

I wrote that sentence as he said it and hated the theater of it. We kept going.

"Router log confirms guest joins by eleven thirty," I said. "Jenna's phone, iPhone-JR, associated at 23:56 and stayed. She had been on our Wi-Fi often. Benji's phone came and went. Conrad's never joined. Erica's sat with Guest from earlier in the week. Margo's tablet had joined last week. Label ME-TAB. Hue received OFF and ON from ME-TAB at midnight. That sits with her lockbox fidgets. I am saying this here because grids like friends."

Havel lifted his book and penciled the three down the margin. Lockbox checks, ME-TAB, OFF ON. His small map started to look like a clean mind.

"Make a roster card," Asa said. "We tape it to the edge of the counter until this case goes downstairs."

I took a thick index card and printed a list:

- 11:10 Erica, seat A, moderator
- 11:12 Margo, seat D, lockbox checks at :20, :43, :58
- 11:18 Conrad, seat C, back door calls 11:41 and 11:53
- 11:20 Benji, seat B, double espresso, croissant intact
- 11:30 Jenna, setup near travel shelf, tea with honey
- 17:05 to 17:45 Rafi floor work travel aisle only
- 17:12 pad pack purchase, one slot later missing

I taped the roster card to the counter lip, then took a photo with the clock above us for anchor.

"Now the key line," Rafi said. He opened a small notebook he keeps for oddities that do not fit their bins. The cover had three coffee rings and a cat hair under the laminate. He flipped to a page with a small note in the margin. Missing pad, drew it at 17:12. Best guess: migrates.

"Where," Asa said.

"Floor, ladder, chair," Rafi said. "Pads sometimes ride until heat loosens them. This adhesive tears clean on the peel when fresh. We will see the pattern on the back if we find it."

"Describe the back," Havel said.

"Two crescent peel scars where you catch the paper and pull," Rafi said. "Clean shine on adhesive. Dust picks up fast if it hits a rug. If the pad rode the aisle for an hour, the back will carry lint on one radius and a clean bite where the foot pressed."

"Good," Asa said. "Find it."

We started with the obvious. Under chairs. Under the low table. Along the chalk curve. Rafi went to hands and knees and used the small LED strip light we keep in the drawer to rake the rug nap. Lint glowed. Threads from a hem glowed. Nothing round glowed where a pad would.

"Rug ate nothing," Rafi said. "Next the blanket in back."

We moved to the back room. The moving blanket had done its job under the ladder while we handled the feet. Rafi lifted the edge and shook it once over the trash sack he had set earlier. Dust fell in a tired gray curtain. One pale circle winked and clung at the hem seam.

"Hold," I said. I steadied the blanket with two fingers.

A thin rubber disk sat half stuck to the fabric seam, adhesive side away. It had the diameter of our peel pads, a hair scuffed on the face, a faint smear of orange wax around one edge where a person at a sales desk would not notice it but a clerk would. On the back, two fresh crescent peel marks showed where a thumb had pulled the paper covers. The adhesive still looked wet in streaks where the rug had not gotten it. The marks were new enough to love.

"Pad," Rafi said. He did not smile. He steadied his breath.

"Photograph," Asa said.

I set the scale card along the hem, kept the pad in place, brought today's paper into the corner of the frame, and shot two. One wide with blanket, one close on the back with the peel scars. I read the minute.

"Time zero nine forty-three," I said. "Peel pad found adhered to moving blanket hem, adhesive side up, fresh peel marks visible, faint wax smear on edge."

Havel bent to look without touching. "Face shows a scuff," he said. "That says it met floor as a pad, not as trash."

"Edge wax says travel aisle," I said. "We will match the cast to the bottle on the shelf if I heat the card again. I am not going to lick a pad for show."

"Please do not," Asa said.

Rafi held a glassine out and I lifted the disk by its rim with tweezers. It did not want to leave the blanket. The adhesive voiced its complaint with a small string. I coaxed it free and laid it in the sleeve face up. The back with peel scars stayed visible. He sealed it. I wrote the card. Peel pad recovered from moving blanket hem, back shows fresh peel crescents, face shows wax edge transfer. I signed. Asa signed. Havel initialed the corner. He liked the corners. I let him have them.

"Chain the blanket sweepings too," Asa said.

Rafi rolled the rest of the dust from the shake into the sack, tied it, and labeled it. Back room blanket sweep, 09:45. He set it near the ladder bag.

"Picture the motion," Havel said. "Pad peeled at five twelve. Pressed to ladder foot. Ladder swung. Pad came half free and rode. It let go when we set the ladder on the blanket."

"Agreed," I said. "The string we saw says it lifted off the fabric clean, which happens with fresh glue. If this pad had lived stuck to a chair for a week, the back would be gray with lint and the peel crescents would not read so new."

"Let me smell the edge," Rafi said, and bent to the glassine like a perfumer. "Citrus," he said. "Bright. Matches the bottle."

I held my test card from last hour near the sleeve and warmed the edge with palm heat. The pad answered with the same thin orange sigh as the bottle. I logged that on the card with one simple line. Warmed adhesive gives citrus odor.

We carried the pad forward to the front and set the sleeve on the counter with the roster card, the till strip, and the sign-in. The pile looked like the truth wants friends.

"Back to arrivals," Asa said, because he never lets a find derail the schedule.

"Benji at 11:20, signed, double, seated," I said.

"Jenna at 11:30, asked for outlet," Rafi said. "I told her none by the shelf. She asked for a stool. I said no. She then set her tote by the map stand. She requested the guest password even though she has it starred in her phone."

"Conrad at 11:18," I said. "Water at 11:41 and 11:53, back door relief calls."

"Margo at 11:12," Rafi said. "Checked the lockbox on a schedule like she was calibrating the room. At :58 she looked at the tablet sleeve in her tote and then at the circle and smiled like the bell belonged to her."

I wrote those last two lines and felt the anger settle in a useful shape.

"Roster gives me placement for the test," Asa said. "Benji stays at B. Jenna at her seat with no rig. Conrad at C with his eyes on the door. Margo at D with her hands where I can see them. We will run the lights at the bell and five past. We will watch the chair go. We will watch arms."

Rafi tapped the counter's edge twice to match the clocks. "We run that when the coroner clears us," he said. "I want the aisle to forgive us before we cut."

"Before we leave the counter," I said, "one more item."

I pulled the small plastic jar we keep by the register that holds the blue painter's tape. On the side, in my hand, I had written a petty note two weeks ago to remind the crew to save a strip of the pad backing when they refresh ladder feet. We tape one to the cabinet door with the date. It keeps us honest about how often we burn through rubber on house jobs. The jar was empty. No strip this week. That fit the missing slot and the pad in the glassine.

I took a photo of the jar and wrote the line on a card. No pad backing saved during 04.14 refresh. Pack shows one missing. Pad located on blanket.

"People will ask why we care about a circle of rubber," Havel said.

"Because the circle knows where it slept," I said.

He smiled once. He does that when paperwork makes poetry by accident.

Rafi set the pad sleeve next to the till strip and anchored both with the stapler. The counter now told a story in three parts. At five twelve we bought the thing. At midnight we scraped the aisle with a foot that had the thing. At nine forty-three the thing came home to a glassine. It was enough.

I turned the sign-in sheet and studied the pen tracks. Erica's name at the top, squared letters that looked like she put her jaw into them. Margo's practiced slope. Conrad's quick spike. Benji's careful print. Jenna's loopy r. I do not pretend to profile from handwriting. I do note how ink behaves. Margo had pressed hard enough to bruise the page beneath. The paper disliked her. The paper and I had reached an agreement.

"Anything else on the roster," Asa said.

"One odd," Rafi said. He pointed to a margin note at 23:50. "Timer check by Rafi, wheel off. I wrote it in the moment because Liora has trained me to love redundancy. That pins me at the hall at ten to. I did not touch anything at the bell."

"You already said it on tape," Asa said. "Now your hand backs your mouth."

"Good," Rafi said. He likes when his habits get applause without clapping.

Peppermint put one paw on the roster card and looked at me with the air of a magistrate who wanted the hearing to move. He had slept through enough of this. He wanted lunch to arrive on schedule. We are not barbarians. We feed our staff.

"We are done here," Asa said. "We go back to the aisle. We will set cones in the corners and run the two cuts. You get two seconds of dark at the bell. You get five seconds to feel shame. You keep your hands where I can see them. Then we stop and we match your lies to the track on the rug."

Margo swallowed. Jenna looked at her tote and then shoved it under the chair with a force that told on itself. Conrad checked the door without moving his head. Benji watched me and did not flinch.

I took the peel pad sleeve in my hand and read the back again. Two crisp crescents where a person's nails had lifted paper at five twelve. A clean bite where the foot had pressed it down at five twenty. A skim of orange on the edge from our aisle. It told everything we needed from it.

"The pad shows fresh peel marks," I said for the page. "I bag it."

CHAPTER 13

Phone Grid

Router admin lives where order writes in numbers. We took it on Asa's laptop so the capture would not argue later about who pressed what. He prefers his own keys. I like that habit.

Rafi slid onto the stool by the cabinet and patched Asa in with a short cable. He brought up the admin page and nodded at me to stand where the camera could see both screen and hands. Peppermint followed us like a small auditor and sprang to the shelf above the rack, tail draped, eyes half shut. Texture, not help.

"Start with what we already know, then deepen," Asa said.

Rafi tapped the bookmark. Router admin, logged under our admin profile. He clicked System Log and scrolled to the window we had marked last night. He did not rush. He let each line breathe.

23:59:54 HueHub group Lights pre-stage OFF from device ME-TAB.

00:00:00 HueHub group Lights OFF command from device ME-TAB.

00:00:05 HueHub group Lights ON command from device ME-TAB.

00:05:00 HueHub group Lights OFF command from device ME-

TAB.

00:05:02 HueHub group Lights ON command from device ME-TAB.

"Midnight and five past," I said. "The dip and the vanity check."

"As written," Asa said. "Now show me the guest cache."

Rafi clicked Clients, then Known Devices. The list sorted by last seen. He filtered for tablet. One line glowed like a fish in shallow water.

Name: ME-TAB
MAC: A0:2B:3C:1D:EE:90
Vendor: Samsung Electronics
First seen: 03.28, 19:12
Last seen: 04.07, 20:41
SSID: Peppermint Cat Guest
AP: FrontBay

"Print," Asa said.

Rafi hit print, and the laser at the counter sang its small chirp. Peppermint watched the sheet slide out and blinked like a clerk who hates showmanship.

"Open the DHCP leases archive," I said.

Rafi shifted to Logs, DHCP, Archive. He pulled the last four weeks. The table loaded with the sober patience of a calendar. He searched by the MAC's last four. EE:90. Three hits. Poetry Night, 04.07. Open Mic, 03.28. One afternoon test, 04.01, short association.

He clicked the first hit. The line read:

04.07 19:39 Lease granted
Client name: ME-TAB
MAC: A0:2B:3C:1D:EE:90
IP: 192.168.1.74
RSSI: -58 dBm at AP FrontBay
SSID: Peppermint Cat Guest
Duration: 01:12:35

"Hear your night," I said. "Poetry Night. Your tablet lived with us for over an hour. Guest SSID. Front Bay access point."

"Context," Asa said, "before people try to play games with three letters and a word that can be anyone."

"Pull the floor cam at 19:39 on 04.07," I said.

Rafi opened the archive from the counter camera. The frame showed the circle space reconfigured for the mic, stools stacked, two rows of chairs, the front bay in view. Time stamp clean. Margo sat in the front row with a slim black sleeve on her lap. She slid a tablet out, checked a screen, and read a poem with good vowels and worse intent. The sleeve's seam matched the one sitting in her tote now. Someone in the second row snapped along. The tape had no sound. It did not need it.

"Freeze at the draw," Asa said.

Rafi stopped the frame at the moment her hand pulled the tablet clear of the sleeve. He zoomed on the seam. Canvas, dark thread, small nick near the zipper pull. I glanced at her tote. Same sleeve. Same nick. People who love control do not throw away cases. They carry them like credentials.

"Print that still," Asa said.

We printed the frame with the time stamp and the small nick. Rafi stapled it to the DHCP excerpt that showed the MAC, the name, the SSID, the time. He laid both on the table like a clean sandwich.

"Now the ARP cache," I said. "Even dead, the network remembers."

Rafi opened Tools, ARP Table, Cached. The line for 192.168.1.74 still held the MAC A0:2B:3C:1D:EE:90. The router had not forgotten the relationship between that IP and that MAC. He exported the table to CSV, printed the page view with the ARP row highlighted, and added it to the pile.

"Vendor OUI lookup," Asa said.

Rafi copied the first three bytes, A0:2B:3C, into the OUI tool bundled in the admin page. Samsung Electronics came up again. He printed that too, not because vendor string changes anything, but because a case likes when small facts sit still.

"Now the Hue hub's user list," I said. "It logs bridges between device labels and user tokens."

Rafi opened the hub interface and navigated to Users. It showed a list of device names that had paired at some point. Liora-Admin. Rafi-Test. ME-TAB. M-E-Phone from a week back. He clicked ME-TAB. The entry showed linked scenes adjusted on 04.07 for a test and on 04.14 for our night. He printed the screen.

"Hue does not log MAC," Asa said.

"It logs label and token," I said. "Router gives us the MAC. Combine both, and you have a person who either owns a tablet called ME-TAB or borrows it every time she walks into my shop and uses it to touch my lights."

Rafi backed out to the Guest SSID settings and pulled the association history. The admin panel keeps ten days of light reporting. Three times for ME-TAB. He overlaid the association on a heat map the panel draws for AP signal strength zones. The dot for 04.07 showed strong FrontBay strength for most of the hour. That dot lived two meters from where Margo sat in the still. The dot for 03.28 showed the same. The dot for the one-minute join on 04.01 sat near the counter, likely a test while she paid for a bookmark set.

"Print the heat overlay with the frame," Asa said.

We did. We circled the dot for 04.07 and the sleeve nick in the still. We dated both and signed the edge. We have learned not to trust staples alone. Ink beats metal when time gets rude.

"Next level," Asa said. "Anything that ties that MAC to her outside this room."

"Bluetooth," Rafi said. "Our little portable speaker keeps a list. It paired to ME-Phone last month, which is her phone. It has seen ME-TAB once. Date 04.07. Pair canceled after the poem set because the speaker was off. The list still holds the name. We can photograph that menu."

"Do it," Asa said.

Rafi tapped through the speaker's menu and held the tiny screen under the document camera. Paired devices: Liora-Admin, Rafi-Lap, ME-Phone, ME-TAB. Last seen dates for each. 04.07 for the tablet. We took the shot. We wrote the card. Shop speaker device memory lists ME-TAB last seen 04.07.

"Now the captive page," I said. "We do not run a login, but we do display a terms screen with a checkbox. People tick it and we keep a line with a time. No personal data. A hash of the MAC and a timestamp. Enough to prove presence, not to sell ads."

Rafi opened the portal log. It showed a hashed MAC that matched the front half of A0:2B:3C via the admin tool's reconciliation function. The hash wrote itself in a clean line. Consent tick at 19:12 on 04.07. The page accepts the same device again without tick within seven days. We printed the thin log.

"Back to midnight," Asa said. "Show me how ME-TAB talks to the hub without joining Guest at the time. We already know the cloud path works. Show the record that it remembered our bridge from a prior join."

Rafi clicked the Hue bridge whitelist again and pointed at the token under ME-TAB. Date created 04.07, time 19:25, IP 192.168.1.74. That is the lease we saw. Once a token exists, the app can call the cloud to control the bridge without having to rejoin our network. He printed that whitelist entry and taped it to the DHCP line like a flip-book.

"Summarize," Asa said.

"ME-TAB joined our Guest SSID on 04.07," I said. "It got IP .74. It paired with our Hue bridge at 19:25 and kept a token. On 04.14 the same label issued OFF and ON to our group at midnight and five past. The router shows the label, and the whitelist shows the token origin tied to the IP and time of the 04.07 join. The cached clients table shows the MAC A0:2B:3C:1D:EE:90 for ME-TAB, vendor Samsung, seen here during the events we just named. Our floor cam still from 04.07 shows Margo reading from a tablet with a sleeve nick that matches the sleeve in her tote tonight. The shop speaker remembers ME-TAB from 04.07. The captive portal log shows a consent tick at 19:12 on 04.07 for a device that reconciles to that MAC."

Havel wrote it in his book the exact way I said it, only with fewer commas.

"Now put a face on ME," Asa said.

We stepped from the rack to the counter. Margo sat in her chair with her tote at her feet, sleeve peeking like a claim on space. I set the prints on the table. DHCP, ARP, whitelist, Hue log, heat overlay, speaker memory, floor cam still. I like the way paper looks when it builds a clean wall.

"Margo," Asa said, voice mild. "At 04.07 you sat in our front row with your tablet. At 19:12 your device joined our Guest network. At 19:25 your app paired to our Hue bridge. Your tablet label is ME-TAB. Tonight at 23:59:54 and again at 00:00:00 and 00:05:00 your tablet label issued OFF and ON to our front bay lights. Our wall wheel was set to always on. The breaker did not move. Your hands checked the lockbox at twenty past, forty-three, and fifty-eight. Your device history shows our bridge on its list. Our router shows your label in its log. Our speaker shows your tablet in its memory. Your sleeve nick matches the sleeve you used last week. Your tote contains that sleeve."

She looked at the prints one at a time. She did not reach to touch. She held her mouth in a line that courts use to cast women who want to be seen as composed. It reads as a straight edge to me.

"I already told you," she said. "I check my lamps at home when I get anxious. If your lights responded, your network takes commands it should not. I do not code. I do not know how bridges work."

"Your app paired to our bridge last week when you read at Poetry Night," I said. "It remembered the bridge. It showed you an option called Peppermint Cat. You chose it. Twice."

She aimed a look at me that is supposed to flay a weaker clerk. I have worked in rare shops since I was tall enough to see over a counter. That look does not cut.

"This proves nothing about intent," she said. "At worst it says I touched the room. I did not kill anyone."

"It proves control and timing," Asa said. "Intent lives on a different line. We are not writing intent here. We are writing a grid."

He tapped the DHCP print with the back of his pen. "What is the name of your tablet," he said.

She kept her voice light. "It is my business."

"Say the name," he said.

"Samsung Galaxy Tab," she said.

"The device name you give it," he said.

She flinched a hair. "ME-TAB," she said. "For Margo Ellsworth. So I know which device is mine in a list."

"Thank you," he said.

She saw how that sounded and pretended to laugh. "Everyone does it," she said. "I could name it Peppermint Pie if that helps you feel less threatened."

"You named your phone ME-Phone," Rafi said, "when you paired to our speaker. It remembers you. It remembered your tablet too. Same night. We took a photo of the menu."

She raised her chin. "So what."

"So the room knows your toys," I said. "And your toys know my lights."

Conrad looked at the door again like it had filed for a restraining order. Jenna watched the prints with bright, hungry eyes. Benji looked at me and then at Margo and looked tired of people who mistake rooms for stages.

"MAC address," Asa said. "Say the last four digits."

"I do not memorize numbers," she said.

"You will recognize them when we put them in your hand," he said. "A0:2B:3C:1D:EE:90. We can put that number in a warrant. We can match it at your house in one visit. We can match it in your bag if you hand me the tablet now."

She slipped one hand toward her tote and stopped, like a fish that sees a net. "My tablet is personal," she said. "You do not get to search me because a log prints a name."

"I asked," he said. "I can ask with paper later. That takes time and eats your sleep. Or you can hand me the device and let the record show you cooperated."

She smiled the way people smile when they decide to gamble. "You can ask with paper," she said. "I will meet you tomorrow at your office with counsel."

Asa did not sigh. He never feeds theater. He nodded as if she had ordered black coffee. "Fine," he said. "We will draft it in an hour."

He turned back to the laptop. "Before we break, tie the five past blip again," he said. "I want the petty vanity captured."

Rafi pulled the Hue log screen and the router event log again and printed a neat band that showed OFF at 00:05:00 and ON at 00:05:02. The lamp dip after the chaos. The kind of tick a person does when they want to feel their thumb over a room.

"Put that strip next to the roster," Asa said.

I did. I wrote a plain line across the bottom. Five past dip suggests post-event check by same device label. He signed under it. He enjoys little needles that do not lose sharpness in court.

"One more," Rafi said. "Guest heat map for last night at 23:58 shows an odd dot near the lockbox. Not ME-TAB. That is an AP blink, not a device. But the dot will confuse anyone who tries to use a picture without reading the caption. We label it now."

He printed the map, drew an X through the AP blink with a red pen, and added the caption. AP channel scan artifact, not client. We will not let a gallery of pictures build a conspiracy where a scan lived.

"Good," Asa said. "Now I want a clean narrative line on this grid in the case file and a short version for the test script."

I opened the binder and wrote:

- ME-TAB label paired to our Hue bridge on 04.07 via IP .74.
- Same ME-TAB issued OFF/ON at 00:00 and 00:05 on 04.14.
- Cached clients table ties ME-TAB to MAC A0:2B:3C:1D:EE:90, vendor Samsung.
- Captive portal shows consent tick at 19:12 on 04.07 for reconciled hash.
- Speaker device list shows ME-TAB on 04.07.
- Floor cam 04.07 still shows Margo with tablet sleeve nick that matches current sleeve.
- Lockbox checks by Margo at :20, :43, :58 on 04.14.
- Wheel set always on. Breaker did not move.

I signed the page and slid it under a plastic guard. I printed a short version for the test sheet and taped it to the back of my clipboard.

"Before we step away," Havel said, "one witness tie outside of logs."

"Gran," I said. "She saw Margo leave Blind Date Night with the last of the cat's-eye. She signed the volunteer slip. She knows Margo's posture when she asks for favors. Tablet or no tablet, the paper and the network stand together."

"Good," he said.

Peppermint yawned and tapped Asa's pen with one soft paw. He dislikes when humans touch plastic for long. He wants cloth and sun and bowls with rules. I cannot argue.

We closed the laptop and took the print stack to the counter, then set every page in sleeves. The Hue strip lay with the router strip and the whitelist and the DHCP chunk and the still. We bridged them with a card that said Device link, log to face. I set the scale card beside the pile and took a single wide photo with the wall clock in frame. I said the time for the room.

"Time ten twenty-two," I said. "Router admin ties ME-TAB to midnight and five past. Cached clients show Peppermint Cat Guest on ME-TAB. MAC matches device seen last week. Hue whitelist shows token created at that earlier join. Floor cam still shows user with the tablet. Speaker memory matches. We print, sign, and file."

Margo watched me clasp the binder. "You are proud of your paperwork," she said.

"I am proud my paperwork keeps people honest," I said. "Even when they forgot how."

She fed a smile to the room and starved it of truth. "Call my counsel," she said to Asa. "He adores prints."

"I will," Asa said. "Now hand me the tablet."

She put both hands on her lap and folded her fingers in a neat square. "Not tonight," she said. "You will get it tomorrow."

Rafi did not say the word stall. He wrote the time in the chain log and drew a small square next to her name. It meant the same thing.

CHAPTER 14

Alibi Crack

The alley keeps our secrets until a lock writes them down. I took Asa and Havel through the stock door, past the crates we keep for book fairs, and out to the strip where the dumpster lives with two stubborn weeds. The air carried wet concrete and the metal tang from the drain that never learned manners. Peppermint watched from the office window and flicked his tail at my back like a metronome. Texture, not help.

Rafi had the smart lock app open before I asked. He held Asa's laptop balanced on one palm and mirrored the phone to it so the capture would not argue later. He knows what a file needs to survive a cross.

"Back door, device name Cat Back," he said. "Admin view."

The log printed itself in tidy rows.

00:01:07 Unlock by code CV-135
00:01:25 Door open
00:01:41 Door closed
00:01:42 Auto-lock engaged
00:01:44 Lock successful

"CV," Asa said.

"Conrad Vale," I said. "Number sequence assigned when he insisted on access to haul event chairs on weekends. He signs for it each quarter. We require codes for vendors and landlords. They hate it until a record saves them from their own mouths."

Rafi tapped the code profile. The screen showed the assignment card. User: Conrad Vale. Code CV-135. Created 01.10. Owner signature on file. Last used 04.14 00:01:07 via keypad. He printed the profile and the event list. The little laser sang inside on the counter and spit truth onto paper.

"Photograph the screen," Asa said. "Then zoom the minute."

I set the scale card on the laptop bezel, brought today's paper into the edge, and shot the log page. Close on 00:01:07. The app's seconds helped. The wall clock inside had given us the rest.

Havel looked at the slab outside the door. The strip showed a thin smear from last night's light rain. Mud had tracked from the drain to the base of the frame and spread a thumb width onto the concrete. He crouched, placed a fresh scale card next to the smear, and nodded me in.

"Heel mark," he said.

I knelt and stayed clear of the patch. The smear carried a single diagonal ridge with a notch on one side, like the bite on a cheap dress shoe. We had seen a twin on Conrad's right heel. It had worn a dull gray with a trace of grit and a hint of wet earlier. Mud does not love carpet. It tells on you when you find concrete again.

"Photograph," I said.

Rafi took two shots. Slab and smear with the door in frame. Close on the ridge. He set the time for the page.

"Time ten forty-nine," I said. "Back door log shows unlock at 00:01:07 by code CV-135, door open and closed within thirty-four seconds. Mud smear outside frame shows single heel pass with diagonal notch. Matches earlier heel mark on Conrad's shoe."

Asa pointed at the keypad. "Smudge pattern," he said.

Rafi angled the flashlight at the digits. Fresh oils leave tiny halos on hard plastic. The five and the one wore a soft cloud. The three had a dull gloss different from the rest. The digits that arrive in a code leave a constellation if you catch them soon enough.

"Photograph the pad," Asa said.

I held the light steady while Rafi shot. He circled the 1, 3, and 5 on a printed copy of the keypad we keep in the maintenance folder. He wrote the time and taped the photo to the diagram.

"Combine with the log," he said, and did. The code 135 matched the pad's blush. He stapled the diagram to the printout with CV-135 in the column.

Havel lifted a small scraping from the mud line with the tip of a tongue depressor and slid it into a vial. "Color and grit," he said. "We can match to the strip if Conrad lets us borrow his heel again. We can match without his permission if the photo we took earlier holds up."

"We swabbed the heel for wax," I said. "We photographed the smear then. We can mark the new scrape line now for range."

He nodded and sealed the vial.

We stepped back inside. Conrad stood two paces from the back hallway entrance as if he had stepped there by mistake and then stayed because momentum ran out. He watched the alley door, not our faces. He had that habit. He would have to lose it.

"Asa," I said, "bring him to the strip."

Asa did not raise his voice. "Conrad," he said. "Back door."

Conrad came with his hands in plain sight. He looked past the lock to the drain and then down at his shoe as if he hoped the floor had changed its mind.

"Air," he said, before anyone asked. "I stepped out for air."

"Time," Asa said.

"Minutes after the lights came up," he said. "I was rattled. I do not do scenes."

Rafi held up the print. "00:01:07," he said. "You used your assigned code. You opened for fourteen seconds and closed at forty-one. Tell me you smoked. Tell me you called. Tell me you said a prayer. Pick the verb that respects the numbers."

Conrad kept his jaw set. "Air," he said again. "You felt that press. Everyone did."

"You used the blackout to lean on her about rent," I said. "Then you stepped out to steady your face."

He looked offended by the noun. People who own buildings prefer words like stewardship. It sits sweeter in their mouths. He had to swallow mine.

"I spoke in a low tone," he said. "No lean."

"You did not touch her," Havel said.

He looked at Havel. "No," he said. "I did not lay a finger on her. Ask the room."

"I am asking you," Havel said.

"I did not touch her," Conrad said again. He made the mistake of saying it too loud. A line like that prefers quiet.

Rafi held up the photo of the keypad blush. "Your code reads one three five," he said. "Pad agrees. Lock page agrees. Slab agrees. Your heel told us as much when you tried to sell me a story about the travel aisle last hour."

Conrad took a breath, short and tight. "I stepped out," he said. "That is all."

"Why," Asa said.

"Because I needed air," he said.

"Why," Asa said again.

Conrad's mouth tightened. "She would not sign anything new," he said. The words hit the wall and stuck like paint.

Silence has a texture. You can smell it when a room pretends to be empty while two sentences try to breathe. He heard his own words and shut his mouth late.

Havel turned the page in his notebook and wrote the line. He did not underline. He did not need to.

"Asa," I said, "log the quote."

Asa set his pen. "Subject states, quote, she would not sign anything new, end quote," he said. He wrote time ten fifty-two next to it without smiling.

Conrad tried to reel it back with posture. It did not help.

"I offered a bridge addendum," he said. "Not a full lease. A memo that would give us time. A thing a court would respect while we negotiate."

"During a blackout," I said.

"I am a moderator of the block's business," he said, like a person who has rehearsed that sentence.

"Erica was moderator of a club, not your block," I said. "You tried to make the two live in one hand. She refused."

He stared past me to the hallway. "She would not sign," he said again, softer. "You people treat paper like a religion when it suits you. I thought a memo might stand in as a hymn."

"Religion has hours," Gran would have said. I let the ghost of her line sit quiet at the back of my throat.

Rafi looked at his watch and read the seconds because he cannot help himself. "You used the cut," he said. "Then you opened the door at 00:01 and took your air. You closed at forty-one and you stood in the frame until the auto-lock engaged."

Conrad's eyes flicked to the line on the print that showed Lock successful at 00:01:44. He nodded once, as if conceding a point in a card game he thinks he will still win.

"Photograph the heel again," Havel said.

Conrad hesitated, then lifted his right foot like an airport passenger. I kept my face blank and got the shot. Fresh mud sat on the notch. You could see the color matched the strip by the drain. In the edge of the notch a thin lighter grit lived, not from our floor, from the alley sand line where the city pretends to clean once a week.

"Time ten fifty-five," I said. "Photo of right heel shows fresh mud with alley grit, diagonal notch matches smear by back door."

Asa placed the lock printout next to the heel photo and photographed the pair. He signed the back with my initials and Havel's. I set a card on the counter for the binder. Back door unlock at 00:01 by CV-135. Door open fourteen seconds. Heel mud matches alley strip. Code assignment card attached.

Conrad watched us sign the paper that turned the sentence in his mouth into an object on my counter.

"I did not hit her," he said.

"I did not ask you if you did," I said.

"You are thinking it," he said.

"I am thinking you tried to buy pressure with time," I said. "And the room sold you something else."

He looked like a man who had swallowed the wrong pill.

"Who did," he said.

"Not your question to ask," I said. "Your piece is the door and the sentence you dropped."

Havel turned back to the hallway. "Put him on the record with his phone," he said to Asa. "Ask for the call log for 00:00 to 00:03. He will refuse. Note the refusal. We will pull a carrier record with paper."

Asa nodded. "Conrad," he said. "Your phone log. Show me calls at midnight."

Conrad pulled his phone out, looked at it, and put it back. "No," he said, with dignity he had not earned. "I will provide a copy through counsel."

"Noted," Asa said. He wrote refusal, phone log, and did not look angry about it. He does not feed pride.

We moved back to the circle. I set the lock print on the table next to the Hue and the router logs. I like when a board holds its nails in one plane. You can frame the night with fewer slips.

"Time ten fifty-nine," I said for the camera. "Alley lock log confirms back door unlock at 00:01 by code CV-135. Code assignment card shows user Conrad Vale. Keypad digits show fresh oils on 1, 3, 5. Heel smear on slab matches shoe. Subject states Erica would not sign anything new. Subject denies contact during blackout. Subject refuses on-scene phone call review."

Peppermint had found a bar of sun on the office sill and was tinting it with his belly. He looked at me with half-lidded approval. Texture only. I took it.

Jenna tried to look relaxed. The strain turned into curiosity and then spoiled into need. "This still does not make him a killer," she said.

"It makes him a person who used a blackout to apply pressure to a woman who was not his employee," I said. "It makes him a person who thinks a back door gives air. It makes him a person whose shoe prints tell us a route."

"You were going to vote," he said, hard.

"We do not vote in the dark," I said. "We count when the room sees our hands."

Margo had her fingers folded and her chin up. She took in the lock print the way a chef watches a rival plate a dish. She looked at Conrad and did not look pleased.

"It was a procedural confirmation," she said, pure sugar.

"It was an attempt to remove the only person who could hold your rent plan in place long enough to choke it," I said. "You printed your ballots on our watermarked stock, fed them through the chamber copier with a ghost ring, and then set your device to dip our lights. You wrote the scene. Conrad tried to improvise a monologue inside it. The night wrote a different script."

I heard myself speak and wanted coffee. Rafi read that thought on my face and went to the kettle like a hero in a quiet play.

Asa set his notebook down and stood in the space that knows trials will never love it. "We have a door," he said. "We have a code. We have a shoe. We have a quote. None of those pick up the ladder. They tell us a man who wanted a signature did not touch the metal that left wax on rubber. They tell us he stood where a back door knows him and took air while a room held its breath."

Conrad swallowed the speech without chewing. "I will sit," he said, and did.

"Before you do," Havel said, "state one more thing. Did you step behind Erica's chair during the cut."

"I leaned," he said. "I spoke in a low tone. I did not touch her, and I did not shove her chair."

"Asa," Havel said, "mark his hand position."

Asa made a small square near the chalk map and wrote no contact claimed. He drew a short line from Conrad's seat toward Erica's shoulder and stopped it before the chair back rail. Then he slid the pen under the photo of the blue fiber in the glassine. He did not need to say it out loud. The transfer we had belonged to another hand.

Rafi poured mugs and set them on the counter without sound. Peppermint lifted his head at the smell and then put it back down. Cats like order. Coffee is keepers' order. He understood.

"Next," Asa said. "We run the blackout test when the coroner clears. Everyone stands where they stood. We cut the lights for two seconds. We watch hands. We listen for scrape. Conrad, you will not lean or speak. You will sit and show me your hands. You will not confuse my room with your hallway."

He nodded without looking offended. His pride had learned something since we opened the door.

I placed the lock print in a sleeve and wrote the card for the file. Alley smart lock, unlock 00:01 by CV-135, code Conrad Vale. Door open fourteen seconds, closed and auto-locked. Keypad shows fresh oil on 1,3,5. Slab smear at threshold matches heel notch. Subject admits stepping out for air. Subject blurts Erica would not sign anything new. Subject denies contact. I signed and handed the pen to Asa. He signed under me. Havel initialed the corner.

The sun on the sill slipped one inch. Peppermint shifted with it and denied the room his attention. He had seen enough people say enough words for one morning.

The night had asked for a villain. The door gave us a man with motive and poor judgment. The floor gave us a ladder that had found wax. The chair gave us a path toward a box. The mic gave us a breath and a word. None of it pointed to Conrad's hand on metal. Enough of it pointed to his mouth near a woman's ear in a dark that he helped want.

I looked at the board of prints and felt the shape settle. Margo held the dip. Jenna fed the scare. Conrad added pressure. Erica sat at the hinge. The ladder did what ladders do under weight and panic. System, not theater. Paper, not opinion.

"Time eleven thirteen," I said for the camera and the counter. "Back door piece placed. We move to test."

CHAPTER 15

Podcaster Panic

The aisle had healed as much as a room can. Cones at the corners. Chalk still faint in the rug. The ladder sat where Asa told me to place it, back in its bag, feet over the moving blanket, a narrow strip of painter's tape marking the exact footprint it had held when we found Erica.

"We do this clean," Asa said. "Two passes. Two seconds in the dark to watch hands. Then the five-second window the hub log wrote for us. No one improvises. No one speaks unless I call on you."

"Phones," I said.

Rafi held the lockbox like a bread tray. Each person walked a phone into it and stepped back. The box shut with a small final click that made the hair at my neck settle.

"Positions," Asa said.

I set chairs in the same arcs we had frozen in photos. Benji at B. Conrad at C with a view to the back door he could not have if he behaved. Margo at D with her tote under her seat, sleeve peeking, hands where we could see them. Jenna at her chair, tote beside her, tripod collapsed on the floor at the inside leg, where her hands had drifted during every setup she had ever pretended was ambience. Rafi at the hall mouth with the router page open on Asa's laptop for the timer cut. I stood at the edge of the circle.

Peppermint took the moderator chair for a moment, flexed his paws, then hopped off and strolled to his post on the counter. Texture, not help. Still right.

"Ground rules," Asa said. "At the word blackout we cut lights. Two seconds. On my count. You do nothing. At the word hold you freeze. Jenna, I will ask one thing of you on the first pass. Put your hands where they went at the bell. No tricks. If your body moves before your mind edits, let it show itself."

She set her jaw. She nodded once. She had already watched her own file betray her. That helps.

"Asa," I said. "Audio."

Rafi had already opened the clip we pulled, the ten seconds from 23:59:58 to 00:00:06. He set the laptop mic near the endcap, not for recording this time, only for comfort. He loaded a simple metronome tick at one beat per second into a tiny speaker on the counter, low enough to guide without turning this into theater. We would run light and body against time. Nothing fancy. The city hates fancy.

"Pass one," Asa said. "Two seconds in the dark."

He looked at Rafi. Rafi tapped the Hue page. The front bay lights softened once as if taking a breath, then cut. The aisle went honest.

"Blackout," Asa said.

One Mississippi. Two.

"Lights," he said.

The bulbs rose back to white. We all stood where we had started. Except Jenna. Her right hand had shot past her chair back and closed on the top segment of the tripod like a habit. Her left hand went to the quick-release near the head. The rig had not fallen because the foot sat on the safe side of the line. Her fingers told us what her mouth would stall.

Asa did not raise his voice. "Hold," he said.

He walked to Jenna's chair and stood where Erica had sat. His shoulder brushed the rail where the pale blue threads had clung. He faced the tripod and measured the distance from her hand to the rig and from the rig to the ladder bag.

"Again," he said. "Slow."

He placed my hands where Erica's had been, on my knees. I am not tall. The geometry still worked. He let the light stay up and had Jenna repeat the reach in daylight. Right hand to the leg. Left to the head. Pull inward, not up. The tripod leaned into the aisle.

"Why there," he said.

"My mic lives on the head," she said. "I was going to cradle it."

"Your mic sat in your tote," I said. "You staged the sound from the map stand. Your hand only knows one story. You reached for a rig because that is how you make panic into content."

She swallowed. She kept her hands on the leg. Her forearm had a tremor she could not hide, the kind that visits when a lie ends.

"Pass two," Asa said. "We run the five seconds. You keep your hands as they were just now. If your body adds movement, let it."

He looked to Rafi. Rafi checked the router, brought up the Hue page, and nodded.

"Blackout," Asa said.

The bulbs cut at the tick.

"One," he said.

The ladder bag whispered on the blanket as air found its skin.

"Two."

Jenna's right hand cinched down on the tripod leg.

"Three."

Her left tugged at the head. The rig rocked. The inside rubber foot kissed the lower shelf. The contact made a tiny mouse squeal. Same pitch I had heard on her file at 00:00:10. It moved hairs up and down my arms like static.

"Four."

The tripod tipped. The inside leg swung toward the ladder bag. If the bag had not been there, the leg would have scythed the space where thighs and knees had been. The leg met the bag's seam and skated along it. The bag slurred on the blanket.

"Five."

Rafi brought the lights up.

"Six."

The bag twisted as if a shoulder had hit a rung. The ladder knocked the shelf. The shelf answered with a note of varnish that lived exactly where the thud bloom began on Jenna's clip. I felt the breath I had heard on the audio at 00:00:03 and hated my own muscle memory for being right.

"Hold," Asa said.

We stood in place. He looked down at the inside foot of the tripod. It left a small crescent print where the rubber met the shelf. The arc matched the mark I had seen with the lamp angled on the lower board when we first froze our night.

"Photograph," I said.

Rafi placed the scale card under the arc and took the shot. He set the camera flat and shot a second angle to catch the ridge pattern in the rubber. Three concentric rings, a shallow nick near the screw point. He looked up at me and nodded. We did not need to say anything. Rubber remembers.

"Bag the head," Asa said.

I slid a narrow sleeve over the tripod head without touching the quick-release. I put another over the inside leg foot. I wrote two cards and taped them to the sleeves. Tripod head and inside foot bagged after reenactment. Foot left crescent arc on lower shelf. I signed. Asa signed. Havel initialed, because he will always love corners.

"Again," Asa said. "Not for art. For the one in a thousand who will ask if we faked the knock. Rafi, line the metronome with the clip beats."

Rafi set the metronome to tick at the same one per second pace and hit play on the ten-second clip without volume. He used the markers we had printed. Tick at 58, cut at bell, drag at three, light at five, thud at six. He held one finger up and moved it through the air as a baton. He hates theater. He loves rhythm when it tells the truth.

"Blackout," Asa said.

We all watched our own bodies not move. Jenna could not. At the tick for three, her hand went the exact centimeter we had seen on screen. At the tick for four, the rig rose and levered. At the tick for six, the ladder bag scraped and the shelf kissed back. You could count your heart against it. I did, and it matched, and I wished for a different job and then remembered my job is not to wish.

"Lights," Asa said.

He waited. He looked at Jenna's hands. He looked at the shelf and at the bag seam. He looked at me.

"Clue," I said.

Rafi brought the light bar, angled it at the lower shelf, and breathed on the arc with his palm to wake any oil so the camera could love it. The crescent we had photographed earlier darkened by a hair. The fresh print from the reenactment sat inside it like a new moon inside an old one. The rings along the foot matched the ridges in the older smear. Same mold. Same batch. Same pattern of scuff on the outer ring. Enough.

"Photograph," I said again.

Rafi shot the pair. He put today's paper in the frame and took one more with my finger pointing to the overlap without touching it. Judges do not like fingers. Jurors love to see scale. We appease both.

"Time eleven thirty," I said. "Reenactment pass two, five seconds, hand reach matches audio markers. Tripod inside foot smudge overlays prior crescent on lower shelf. Bagged foot and head."

Havel had watched all of that with his mouth still. Now he lifted the corner of the bag seam with a pen tip and looked at the skid mark along the fabric. Orange cast. Thin. From the earlier wax transfer. The kind that migrates when a thing grazes another thing that grazed your aisle.

"Note it," he said.

I wrote the small line on a card. Bag seam shows drag line with faint wax cast after reenactment. I taped it to the bag. I will not give a defense attorney a chance to say my words lived only in my head.

Asa stepped back to Jenna. "You reached for your tripod in the cut," he said. "Not your chair. Not a neighbor's hand. Your rig."

"I panicked," she said.

"You prepared," he said.

She did not answer. Her mouth wanted to. Her eyes found the map stand. Her throat worked.

"Why," he said. "Say the part you practiced. Do not make me tease it out of the air like smoke."

She looked at the sleeve on the tripod head and the one on the foot and realized that this night had stopped being hers to narrate.

"I needed a bump," she said at last. Quiet. "The show goes flat if it is all readings and light tea. I wanted a breath. A sound. A scare people could talk about without anyone being harmed."

"You staged a jump when the lights cut," I said. "You liked the bell. You reached for the rig. The foot kissed the shelf. The ladder went. A head met a rung. We matched the prints to your foot and the bag to the aisle."

"I did not mean harm," she said. Her voice was climbing in pitch and she caught it and shoved it back down. "I have a rule. No injury on tape."

"You broke your own rule," Asa said. "Not because you tried to. Because rooms are not your studio."

She stared at the lower shelf and blinked. She did not cry. Good. I could not be patient if she had.

Rafi brought the laptop with the clip and held it where she could see the markers without hearing the sound. He could have played it. He did not. She already had the pattern in her bones.

"At fifty-eight, the ladder squeaks," he said. "At zero three, we hear the chair drag and the breath. At zero five, our bulbs rise. At zero six, we get the thud. Your hand does what it always does. It loves a lever. The room hated that love."

She pressed her forefinger to her lips like a person who wants to turn time backward with a touch. Time does not take notes from fingers.

"Say it clean," Asa said. "What did you do when the lights cut."

"I reached for my tripod to juice downloads," she said, each word clipped as if she were punctuating with teeth. "I thought a thump would make people keep listening. I did not see her. I did not know the ladder would swing. I did not know the aisle had wax. I did not know."

"You knew enough," I said. "You knew you had staged scares before. You knew chaos pays you."

She looked like a person who wants to ask for mercy and knows the ask will not land.

"Turn your tote," Asa said.

She slid it out with one toe and pushed it open with two fingers. He did not reach in. He set his pen under the flap and lifted the top layer. Mic. Dead cat windscreen. Two rubber bands. One spare foot for the tripod, new and still in its plastic. He looked at the spare and then at the foot we had bagged. Same ridges. Same nick on the outer ring, cast from the same mold defect.

"Photograph," I said.

Rafi took the shot and printed it. We did not need it to prove anything. We did it anyway. Habits save cases.

"Again, for the record," Asa said. "Say it."

"I staged a scare," she said. "To juice downloads."

"Panic followed," I said.

She nodded, once, with an honesty that arrived too late to be brave. "Panic followed," she said.

Conrad let out a sound between a breath and a curse that I did not bother to write down. Margo did not move. Her eyes stayed on the ladder bag as if willing it to hold still would undo physics. Benji looked at the floor and then at me and then at Jenna with the kind of pity that is not kind. Peppermint sneezed from the counter and went back to sleep.

Asa wrote her sentence in his book and underlined only juice downloads. He does not decorate. He wants his future self to find the hook by sliding a fingernail under it.

"Charges later," he said. "Now we finish the test."

He put Jenna back in her seat and made her place her hands in her lap. He made Margo keep hers where the camera could love them. He made Conrad sit back and set his heels flat so no one could mistake footfalls for new motion. He looked at Benji and spared him instruction. Benji already understands rooms.

"Third pass," Asa said. "No one moves. No reaching. Rafi, lights."

The bulbs cut. Two seconds of dark. Four more. No scrape. No foot kiss. No bag whisper. Only air. At five, the lights came back. At six, nothing hit. That silence felt heavier than any thud.

"Thank you," Asa said. "That will keep a prosecutor from having to explain your reach to a juror who thinks panic excuses physics."

He looked at the shelf again and at the crescent prints, old and new, nested like crescents always do.

Havel lifted his head, satisfied in the way a person can be when the math and the blood and the paper consent to be seen together.

"Bag the lower board," he said.

"You want the whole shelf," I said.

"The lower board only," he said. "We will replace it. This is the night's ledger."

Rafi fetched a driver and backed out four screws. We slid the board into a long sleeve and taped each end. I wrote the card. Lower shelf board, travel aisle, carries tripod foot smudge old and reenactment overlay. I signed. Asa signed. Havel initialed.

"Time eleven forty-two," I said. "Blackout reenactments complete. Two-second pass shows reach, five-second pass aligns with markers and thud window. Tripod foot smudge overlays prior mark on lower shelf. Jenna admits staging a scare to juice downloads. Panic followed."

Jenna watched me write that last line on the board's label. She opened her mouth, then closed it. She did not ask to change a word. She did not get to.

Asa looked at Margo and then at Conrad. "We are not done with you," he said. "But the floor has told me enough about the hit."

Conrad set his jaw like a person hearing a verdict that is not his name and still burns his pride. He kept his eyes off the door. Progress.

Margo finally let her hands leave her lap. She pressed her palms flat on her knees as if to iron them. "This is a tragedy," she said.

"This is a room that refused to be your stage," I said. "We will let it breathe now."

Rafi moved the cones and taped the No entry card, then wrote a note for the morning crew and stuck it at the espresso station. Test complete. Shelf bagged. Do not clean the line where the crescent shows. Replace board after release.

Peppermint jumped from the counter to the map stand, sniffed the spot where the mic had sat, and sneezed again with the comic and cruel timing only cats own. He looked at Jenna with a slow blink that did not forgive.

Asa stacked the sleeves and clips and prints, then set the pad with the markers on top. He wrote the time on the front of the case binder. He capped his pen with the tidy click that ends a section.

"No more blackouts," I said.

"No more blackouts," he said.

We stood a moment longer in the travel aisle, the way people do when a room has confessed and still has something to ask.

"Reset your rules," Havel said. "You will write the sign."

"I will," I said. "No secret ballots. No blackouts. No off-network devices."

Peppermint chirped once, approved, and went hunting for the one sliver of sun left on the sill.

CHAPTER 16

New Member Past

Upstairs, the office kept its calm. The glass box held light like a jar. The laser warmed up with a thin whine that said it was ready to turn doubt into paper. Peppermint hopped to the file cabinet and tucked his paws. Texture only. No counsel.

Rafi slid into the chair and woke the desktop. Asa stood, notepad closed for once, hands in his pockets. Havel took the corner spot by the safe where he can watch a screen and a face without picking a favorite.

"Inbox," I said.

Rafi had sent two messages before dawn to Ashmead County Public Library. One to the branch manager address on their site. One to a name I knew from a grants list, a veteran who keeps Friends sales on schedule and volunteers from eating the shelves. We asked for three items. Confirmation of a club split. Any record of disturbances. Any note that older jackets reached their Friends sale with pockets and cards intact.

The desktop chimed. New mail showed in bold. Subject line plain as a ledger: Re: Inquiry, club split and jackets.

"Open it," Asa said.

Rafi clicked.

Dear Ms. Wren,

Thank you for writing. I am the adult services librarian here, and I was in the room during the Ashmead Readers split in 2021. There was shouting and a walkout. No assault, no physical contact. We filed an incident note for volume only.

We ran a Friends sale the month after. Several boxes of jackets left over from a display went to the donation nook. Some still had pockets. Volunteers were instructed to remove cards, which often slip behind the flap. We do not catch every one. Our coordinator remembers a Benji Hsu who resigned during that split and emailed me a clear statement that he wanted his name off the roster. He donated jackets for an art project months later. No ban. No incident. I attach a PDF of the incident note and a scan of the donation ledger entry that mentions jackets with pockets.

Regards,
Maren Doss
Adult Services Librarian
Ashmead County Public Library

Below sat two attachments. Incident_Note_2021-05.pdf. Donation_Ledger_Jackets_2021-09.pdf.

Rafi downloaded both to the case folder and mirrored them to the evidence drive. Checksums on each. He called the hashes out. I wrote them. He opened the first PDF.

One page. Library header. A short form with boxes and lines. Date 2021-05-12. Event Ashmead Readers monthly meeting. Summary: Raised voices regarding curation and access policies, one member used sarcasm that was not helpful, two members left early, one resigned via email. No physical contact, no threats, no calls to police. Note ended with a line I loved: Room cleared in ten minutes, tables reset, circulation resumed. Signed M. Doss.

"Photograph screen and print," Asa said.

I set today's paper in the corner of the frame, snapped the screen with the scale card against the bezel, then printed. Rafi clamped the page with a staple and signed the bottom. I signed under him. Havel initialed the corner because he likes corners.

Second PDF opened to a scan of a ruled page with pencil lines, Friends Sale Donations, September 2021. Entry: Jackets, mixed, 1 banker's box, source BRANCH CLOSET and INDIVIDUAL DONOR, note Pockets present in some, cards removed to shred bin. Two lines down: Donation by Hsu, B., jackets for art, 1 half box, mylar on several, volunteer note "pull pockets when time allows." Initials MD. It sat on the page like a quick memory that decided to pay rent.

"Print," Asa said.

We printed it and set it by the first. Rafi laid the Ashmead email under both, then printed the email header as a separate page for chain. He added each sheet to sleeves, labels at the top like neat collars. Peppermint flicked an ear as if the measuring bored him, then circled and loafed on the staplers.

"Read the language again," Havel said.

I read it. Shouting. Walkout. No assault. Card removal imperfect. Jackets at sale. Benji resigned without drama, donated later, no ban. Everything we needed to cut a branch without sawing into a hand.

"Forward the thank you," I said.

Rafi typed a clean reply. Thank you for clarity. We are handling a club night here. Your files help us trim noise. He sent it and then saved a PDF of our reply for the chain. I like to archive gratitude. It pays back when a clerk has to show a path of respect.

Asa took the incident form and held it in both hands like a prayer card. "This dissolves the specter," he said. "People love a history of rage when they want a villain. No strike then, no strike now."

"Benji's card lived under a jacket flap for years," I said. "Our sleeve shows the pocket shadow. The stamp reads 2017. The ledger here shows pockets linger in that system. The donation entry shows a batch with pockets at Friends and a later half box from Benji. This is tidy without asking anyone to perform."

Rafi pulled the email Benji sent that night to the branch manager, the one he had promised us. It had arrived thirty minutes earlier while we ran the aisle test downstairs. Subject line as promised: I walked away. He had written, short and straight, that he did not want his name used to sell shame. He thanked the librarian for hosting, said he would return books on time, and asked to be left out of future messages. He copied no one. He swore at no one. He had put his name on an exit with care. He had attached a photo of the jackets in his trunk from that later half box. Mylar gleamed in the flash. The flaps sat tucked.

"Print it," Asa said.

We did. I read his line out loud. "I will not treat rooms as stages," he had written then. I let it live in the air. The irony did its job without smirks.

"Bring him up," Asa said.

I stepped to the stairs and called Benji by name. He stood from the circle and came without making the floor feel like it owed him an apology. He took in the office with one slow look, then set his hands on the chair back the way a man sets his hands when he knows he will be asked to meet a mirror.

"We reached Ashmead," I said. "The librarian remembers the split. She confirms loud and not kind. She confirms no violence. She confirms your resignation by email. She confirms jackets with pockets at Friends. She confirms your later half box. We have the scan. We have your photo. Your card in our sleeve rides with a date six years old. It belongs to that era, not tonight."

He breathed once, a thin in and a steady out. "Thank you," he said.

"This trims a branch," Asa said. "I am stating it so the room does not try to grow it back later. You are not our strike. Your name on a card under a flap is history only."

Benji nodded. His face did not change. His shoulders lowered a hair. That quarter inch looked like a person who had put down a bag he had carried alone.

"I stayed quiet too long," he said. "When the card came out of that jacket I shut my mouth to keep from spitting. I do not like being a red herring."

"You handled it with fewer words than some," I said. "You gave us chain. You did not pitch a scene. You let paper do the job."

He tilted his head at the printouts. "I owe the librarian an apology for dragging her back here," he said.

"I wrote the thank you," I said. "Send your own if you want. She will appreciate it."

He watched Peppermint blink at him like a magistrate. Peppermint held the stare for three heartbeats, then shifted his attention to the laser tray as if to say, witness dismissed.

"Sit," Asa said. "Stay with the club. We need people who know when to walk away and when to hold a chair."

Benji pulled in air as if he planned to argue, then thought better and nodded. "I will," he said. "I will also take Tuesday inventory as promised."

"You will," I said.

Rafi stapled the Ashmead email, the incident form, the ledger scan, and Benji's trunk photo to a divider labeled Ashmead, 2021. He slid the stack into the binder between the ballot section and the ladder section so any person who tried to tie those threads would have to touch this page and change their mind.

Havel wrote one line in his book. Branch trimmed. He underlined it and drew a short slash under the underline. He does that when a suspicion deserves burial rather than a plaque.

"Record the minute," Asa said.

"Time eleven fifty-one," I said. "Ashmead librarian confirms club split in 2021 with raised voices, no physical contact. Friends sale carried jackets with pockets. Cards not always removed. Benji resigned by email. Later donated half box of jackets with mylar. Card under jacket flap at Peppermint Cat dates to 2017. No new clues. Branch trimmed. Benji remains."

Rafi sealed the two PDFs to the evidence drive with redundant labels. He wrote the hashes on the sleeve edges, then wrote the numbers in the chain log. He is the only person I know who can make hex feel human.

Benji looked at the window, the sill, the office door, the desk, because men in rooms tend to take an inventory of exits when a room forgives them. Then he looked at me, steadier.

"I am sorry for going quiet downstairs," he said. "I did not want to lawyer the air. It read like a trap."

"Silence can read as guilt when the night is loud," I said. "Say a sentence next time. Make it boring and truthful and end it with an offer to help. Clerks love boring."

He gave a small smile. "I will practice," he said.

"Good," I said. "Sit back in B. Drink the espresso you paid for. Eat the pastry."

"It is stale now," he said, his first attempt at a joke.

"Stale feeds a point," I said. "Go."

He went.

Asa looked at the ceiling as if counting the nails that keep it off our heads. "One less story line to babysit," he said.

"People raise ghosts because ghosts do not sue," I said. "We put this one back in its box."

He shut his notebook and set it on the laser, which scolded him with a warm hum. He moved it to the counter and rubbed the lid with his palm as if to apologize to a machine.

"Before we go down," Havel said, "recite the tree."

I did.

"Margo held the dip and the paper. Jenna staged a scare that turned into a hit. Conrad leaned on Erica in the dark and stepped to the door, but did not touch the ladder. Benji's card is history. The ladder met wax on our aisle. The tripod touched the lower shelf. The chair path turned toward the box. The hub log fixed the seconds."

He nodded. He does not need long speeches when a list can carry weight.

Rafi closed the inbox and set a flag on the Ashmead thread that reads reply sent. He took the incident PDF and scribbled a margin note for my eyes only. Room cleared in ten minutes, tables reset. He likes that as much as I do. It says librarians remember to reset rooms even after a storm. It says we will get to wipe down shelves when this ends. That sentence is the reason I still run a shop in a city that keeps daring me to stop.

Peppermint stretched, reached a paw toward my office keys, thought about batting them again, remembered he no longer has that privilege because of the shelf, and withdrew. He curled, eyes on the staplers, and purred once, quiet.

We walked back down. The circle sat where we had left it. The cones marked the aisle. The bagged ladder lay still. The board with the crescent prints leaned in its sleeve against the counter like a ledger waiting for a signature.

Benji took his seat at B and put the stale croissant on a napkin. He did not eat it. He set his palms on his knees and gave me a small nod that said he would answer questions with sentences now, not silence. That is all a clerk wants from a witness who is not a suspect.

Margo looked at the ceiling, at the Hue bulbs, at the chandelier that has never once cared about modern theatrics. Jenna stared at her hands. Conrad rubbed the edge of his shoe against the rug to clean a line of grit, then stopped when he saw Havel's eyes.

"Status," Asa said.

"Benji is clean," I said. "Ashmead confirms. He stays."

Jenna lifted one hand as if to ask what that had to do with her. She let it fall. Good instinct for once.

Rafi taped a small card to the counter with two sentences on it for the morning crew. Ashmead email filed. Jacket card is history. He lined the edges and pressed the tape flat, an act that calmed me more than coffee.

I took one last photo for the case binder. Benji in seat B with his hands on his knees, the circle in frame, the roster card taped to the counter, the pad sleeve with peel crescents, the board sleeve with the crescent smudge, the stack of Ashmead prints under a paperweight shaped like a cat. Today's paper sat in the corner. I said the time for the log.

"Time eleven fifty-nine," I said. "Branch closed."

Peppermint blinked and approved in silence. He keeps the room honest without language. I do my best to match him with paper.

CHAPTER 17

Vote Motive

The office collects truth with the patience of a clerk. Glass, a cheap laser, a printer that never smiles, cables where they belong. Asa stood where the camera sees his hands. Rafi took the chair. Peppermint hopped to the file cabinet, loafed, and blinked like a bored auditor.

"Queue first," Asa said. "Then her words. Then her tablet."

Rafi woke the admin pane. He had our local logs. He also had a live session with city IT, a woman named Yara who treats spoolers like ledgers. She joined by secure screen. No chatter. She typed with the rhythm of a metronome.

"Print service events," I said.

Rafi brought up the Windows event log for PrintService Operational. Yara filtered to 21:50 through 22:10. Lines stacked into a ladder of certainty.

22:02:11 Document Printed
User: FrontDesk
Document Name: MRC_Procedural_Vote_Moderator.pdf
Printer: Cat-Laser-1
Size: 1,247,512 bytes
Pages: 25
Duplex: False

Client Machine: Cat-Front
Port: USB001

Yara drilled into the event payload. She pulled the job's RenderedDocPath. We had it from earlier, but this time the path came with a bonus. \Device\HarddiskVolume3\Users\FrontDesk\AppData\Local\Temp\fp_render\MRC_Procedural_Vote_Moderator.pdf. She exported the XML to a flat file and read the SHA-256 of the rendered spool. Rafi wrote the hash into the chain log.

"USB mount," Yara said. Her voice through the speaker held no sentiment, only timestamps.

Rafi opened the System log and filtered for Kernel-PnP. 21:59:08. Device USBSTOR\Disk&Ven_Generic&Prod_Flash_Disk&Rev_8.07\1309073000001234. Friendly name UNTITLED. Volume mounted. 22:03:02. Volume ejected.

"Photograph the screen," Asa said.

I set today's paper in the corner of the frame and shot the event panel with the two lines highlighted. I took a close crop on the serial. The laser spit two prints. Rafi signed the bottom of each. I signed under him. He stapled them to the earlier queue capture from last night and to the PostScript header we had pulled with the Author field. M. Ellsworth. We did not have to say that name. It sat in the ink.

"SNMP page count," Yara said. "Between 21:50 and 22:10 the printer's counter advanced by twenty-five. No other jobs of that size hit. You can anchor by the printer's own mind if someone yells about spoofed logs."

Rafi pulled the web panel for Cat-Laser-1. Supplies, Maintenance, Totals. Page count delta matched the job count. He printed the panel. He laid it next to the event print and wrote a plain line. Device counter confirms twenty-five sheets at 22:02.

"Spool header again," Asa said. "Short."

Rafi opened the spool file in hex view and scrolled to

the PostScript header we captured earlier. Title: Midnight Reading Club Procedural Vote, Moderator. Author: M. Ellsworth. CreateDate: 2024-04-14 21:58:13. Producer: Quartz. He printed the header and taped it to the event page so any juror with a finger could follow.

"Now her words," I said. "We tie motive to paper."

Rafi opened the club platform and navigated to the cloud folder where moderators keep pinned documents. He had export rights on our own room. Margo's account had posted a "Process Note" three days ago. Title: Moderator Continuity and Confidence Vote. The first line carried the header phrase, word for word, that sat on the ballots. Midnight Reading Club Procedural Vote, Moderator, Keep or Remove. The footer read Outcome without spectacle. The PDF icon showed under it with her user name and a timestamp. 10:02 p.m. tonight, the same minute our queue finished chewing paper.

"Open the doc," Asa said.

We did. The header font, the thin rule, the tiny cat icon. Identical to the ballot. The platform recorded the file's internal properties in a sidebar. Author M. Ellsworth. Source device ME-TAB. Upload 22:01. Rafi printed that sidebar. He shot the screen with scale and paper, then we signed and sleeved it.

"Screenshot her post from the chat," I said. "The one where she rehearsed the line."

Rafi pulled the thread from the day Conrad floated the rent memo. Margo's post: midnight vote, paper ballots to protect feelings. The tiny graphic under it used the same header. We had printed it earlier. He placed it with the new cloud doc print, the queue, and the spool header and made a spread that read without a narrator. She said the line. She built the file. She fed the printer. She brought the stack to the room.

"Timer app," Asa said. "Tablet."

He walked to the circle. Margo sat with her tote tucked tight to her ankles. The sleeve peeking. The small nick near the zipper.

He set the print stack on the counter and spoke to her the way he orders water.

"Margo," he said. "Open your tablet. Open your Hue app. Show me the bridge list."

"I already told you," she said. "I use the app for my house."

"You stalled," he said. "Now you will show me your screen or we will wait for paper at my office. If you show now, the record will reflect cooperation. If you stall again, the record will reflect that too."

She weighed the room and her options and misjudged both. She opened her tote, pulled the sleeve, and slid the tablet free. She swiped to wake it, thumbed the open, and tapped the Hue icon with a confident little flick that said she had done this motion a thousand times.

The app opened to the tab she used last. Not her house. A bridge list. First line, at the top, Peppermint Cat. The app had saved the child icon I named because branding sells bulbs. Under it, her house bridge. A little home glyph. She swallowed and tried to scroll before anyone saw. Asa's palm hovered an inch from her screen as a boundary. He did not touch. He did not need to. She froze.

"Photograph," I said.

Rafi brought the document camera on its arm, angled it over the tablet, and shot the bridge list with the Peppermint Cat line in clean focus. Today's paper sat in frame. He printed, I signed, Asa signed. He shot one more when she tapped Peppermint Cat and landed on a scene list that showed Front Bay Lamps. The app UI kept a little cache icon next to our bridge name. I liked that little circle more than I like cake.

"Back," Asa said.

She backed out. The bridge list stayed on screen with our shop at the top. Her jaw tightened. She put the tip of her tongue behind her teeth, a small tell she had when control slipped.

"Timer," Asa said. "Show your routines."

She tapped Routines. A bedtime for her house. A morning at seven. A custom called Test 5min. Under each, the target icons. Two had the house lamp glyph. Test 5min had the Peppermint Cat icon. It showed a toggle time at 00:00 and another at 00:05. She let out a sound in her throat that wanted to pretend it was a cough.

"Photograph," I said.

Rafi shot the routine list, then the detail screen when Asa said open Test 5min. It showed a group target. Front Bay. It showed the on and off times. Midnight, five past. She stabbed at the screen like stabbing would change ink. It did not.

"This proves a test," she said. "Rafi asked me to help at a poetry night last week. We were changing dim levels."

Rafi did not give her the dignity of a response. He pointed at the created date. 04.07. He pointed at the last run date. 04.14 00:05:02. The app recorded its own guilt.

"Photograph," I said again. We did.

"Now the tote," Asa said.

Her eyes hardened. She closed the routines pane and tried for flippant. "You cannot search my bag," she said. "You said so earlier."

"I asked you to open your tablet," he said. "You did. Now I am asking you to open your tote and remove loose paper. If you refuse here, I will seize the bag with paper in an hour. Choose your version."

She lifted the tote, set it on the counter, and pulled the sleeve out again as if sleeves satisfy warrants. Beneath it sat a thin folder and a half-inch sheaf of letter stock in a clear pocket. The top sheet blinked a faint oval when the office light hit it. Cat's-eye, right where Gran said the mark lives. The package wore a rubber band that had that dry tack you feel on stock that saw last summer and liked being indoors.

"Set the paper on the desk," I said.

She did, slow.

Rafi gloved up and flipped the top sheet to the light. The cat's-eye winked in the same spot we had mapped. He sniffed. No coffee smell like the chamber glass ring. Clean. Untouched today. He set a scale card on the corner and photographed the stack from above with the mark in frame. He slipped two sheets into a sleeve and labeled them. Cat's-eye sheets, from tote of M. Ellsworth, 04.14. He signed. I signed. Asa signed.

Margo clutched the sleeve like a person who wants to pull rank and has none.

"I do community work," she said. "I carry paper. This is old stock from a shop event. Gran signed me out."

"She did," I said. "She wrote the time. She kept the wrapper and a sample in her garage. Your slip sits in my binder with her stamp. She remembers the night you took the full sheets. You have carried them since August and used them to run secret ballots against a moderator who stopped a rent plan. Then you dipped my lights with a routine called Test 5min."

She raised her chin. "It was a procedural vote," she said.

"Your posts say remove Erica," I said. "Not confirm. Your cloud doc carries the same language as your post. Your PDF prints at 10:02. Your token on the Hue bridge dates to last week. Your app lists Peppermint Cat on top. Your routine shows our group. Your tote carries the last of the ream. Your phone label and tablet label both start with ME. Your lockbox checks lined up with the dip. That is not procedure. That is motive with props."

She looked at the pile. She looked at me. She looked at Asa and tried to measure his patience. He kept his face set at neutral. He can do that longer than anyone I know.

"IT is done," Yara said in our ear, quiet and final. "I have emailed the signed export of the queue and event logs to your case mailbox. I will box the spool file and ship a copy to evidence. Your printer's page count remains intact. Your DHCP, ARP, and whitelist prints match each other. If anyone tries to claim a replay attack, call me. I will write the affidavit."

"Thank you," I said.

Rafi saved Yara's email to the case folder and printed the chain page she attached. He slid it under a sleeve and set it next to the rest. Peppermint cracked an eye, judged the stack's symmetry, and allowed it to live.

"Now we read her post into the air," Asa said. "Out loud."

I opened the chat capture from earlier and the new cloud doc side by side. I read the header. Midnight Reading Club Procedural Vote, Moderator, Keep or Remove. I read the line about Outcome without spectacle. I read the time of her upload. 22:01. I read the printer queue line. 22:02. I read the Hue routine created last week and run tonight. Midnight. Five past. I did not change tone. It did not need color.

"Timer grid, paper grid, post grid," Havel said. "Lock them."

We taped the cloud doc print to the queue print and the Hue routine shot to the router log strip. We taped the cat's-eye tote shot to Gran's volunteer slip copy. We put all three spreads in a row on the office desk and photographed them as one. Today's paper in the corner. Wall clock in frame. I wrote the minute.

"Time twelve twenty-three," I said. "IT export confirms 22:02 queue. Margo's cloud doc at 22:01 with identical language. Hue routine Test 5min shows Peppermint Cat group cached and toggled at 00:00 and 00:05. Cat's-eye sheets recovered from her tote. Motive sits on paper."

Margo had gone quiet. She has two gears. Speech with syrup. Silence with knives. She had switched to silence and the knives were duller than she liked.

"Downstairs," Asa said. "Bring the spreads. Bring the tote photograph. Bring two sheets from her pack for mark comparison. Do not leave the rest on my desk."

We carried the work to the counter. The circle watched without commentary. Jenna stared at the routine shot and saw the word Test reflect in her own mess. Conrad studied the door again and then forced his eyes forward, learning a new trick in public. Benji's hands rested on his knees. Peppermint trotted ahead like a bailiff in fur.

I set the three spreads on the table in front of Margo's chair. I set the sleeve that held two cat's-eye blanks next to them. I added the bottom blank from the ballot stack we had already bagged, the one with the chamber copier ring ghost. I laid a scale card across both so the marks would play together when we shot the pair.

"Light," I said.

Rafi tipped the lamp so the watermarks blinked on command. The cat's-eyes nested. Placement matched. The chamber ring ghost lived on the old bottom blank and not on her tote sheets. I said the sentence into the room so no one could outtalk the photograph later.

"Her tote sheets carry the cat's-eye mark from Gran's ream, placement identical," I said. "Our bottom blank carries the chamber ring ghost, not her tote sheets. The filled ballots carry the same ghost. The PDF header matches her chat post. The queue hits at 22:02. The app routine with Peppermint Cat cached toggled my lights at midnight and five past."

Asa watched Margo's mouth, not her hands. He wanted the tell that costs a person nothing and still gives them away. She met his eyes as if to prove something unnameable, then glanced at the ballots, a quick flick with a recoil at the end. Small tell. She could not help it.

I lifted the stack of ballots we had sleeved earlier, a half inch of paper that thought it was theater. I set the stack on the table in front of her seat. I did not drop it. I did not slam it. I placed it the way a clerk places a ledger. Square and sure.

Her eyes flicked again. Down to the stack. Up to Asa. Over to the crowd. She smoothed her skirt with flattened palms and did not reach for the paper. Good. I do not like slaps.

"End of motive section," Asa said for the camera, voice flat. "We move to charges when the coroner clears the aisle and my phone rings."

He did not look at Margo when he said it. He looked at the lamp, at the Hue strip, at the routine time stamp. Paper raised the room and set it down. My job is to keep it set.

Peppermint hopped to the ballot table, sniffed the stack once, sneezed his contempt, and sat beside it like a small stone with whiskers. He blinked at Margo without malice. Texture only. Truth did the rest.

CHAPTER 18

Full Scene

We bring the room back to order. Chairs where they were when the clock struck. Cones at the corners of the travel aisle. The bagged ladder on the moving blanket. The lower shelf board sealed and leaning by the counter like a page we pulled from a ledger. Peppermint inspects each prop with the seriousness of a tiny bailiff, then takes his post on the register light. Texture only. He refuses promotion.

"Phones," I say.

Rafi holds the lockbox. Everyone drops in their rectangles of nerve. Lids close. Click. He flips the key onto the ring and lays it where the camera can see it.

"Ground," Asa says. "Two passes. First, two-second blackout to mark hands. Second, explain and admit. No speeches. If you want words on the record, you will answer what I ask and stop."

He does not raise his voice. The room raises its attention for him.

I hand the roster card to the lens and speak the positions again so the frame becomes a map anyone can follow later. Erica's chair sits empty, marked with a tag. Then clockwise. Margo in D with her tote under the seat, sleeve peeking, two cat's-eye blanks in a labeled sleeve on the table in front of her. Conrad in C with both heels planted. Benji in B with his palms on his knees, the stale croissant intact as an exhibit on a napkin. Jenna in her chair, tripod collapsed where her hand found it before, head and inner foot bagged after our earlier pass.

"Hue ready," Rafi says from the hallway. Asa's laptop shows the admin page and the markers we printed. The clip sits cued at 23:59:58. The metronome rests, silent. We will not need it to count this time.

"Blackout," Asa says.

Rafi taps. Lights cut. The night in this room is honest and brief. Two heartbeats. Lights climb back. We all stand in our exact outlines except for the reflex Jenna cannot smother. Her right hand floats at the tripod's top segment for the blink before her mind drags it back. We all see it. We have already photographed it. Today I let it be a small mercy and not a trap.

"Thank you," Asa says. "Hold those bodies in your heads. Now the one-pass chain."

He turns his notebook so the camera can see the first line. He writes while he speaks. He always does. Ink makes the air keep its promises.

"Paper first," he says. "Liora."

I slide the spread across the center table. On the left, Gran's volunteer slip with the cat's-eye stamp. On top of it, the wrapper sample she kept with the winking mark. On the right, the cloud post from Margo's account at 22:01, same header as the ballots. Under that, the printer queue at 22:02, with the spool header where Author reads M. Ellsworth and the device counter that climbed by twenty-five. Under that, two blanks from her tote with the mark in the same spot. Then the bottom blank from the ballot stack with the chamber glass coffee ring ghost.

"Watermark from Gran's ream," I say. "Placement matches. Shop held no whole sheets after Blind Date Night. Volunteer slip shows you signed out the last of the stock at 22:50 that night for club use. Tonight your cloud doc lands at 22:01. Your PDF prints at 22:02. Your tote still carries marked sheets. The bottom blank from the ballot stack carries the chamber ring ghost, not your tote sheets. The filled ballots carry that ghost. Chain is closed."

Margo looks at the spread as if words might rearrange the paper if she stares hard enough. They do not.

"Say what you did with the ballots," Asa says to her. "Simple."

"I designed and printed a procedural vote," she says. "To remove a moderator who had lost confidence." Her tone reaches for neutral and trips on conviction.

"On our shop's leftover stock signed out to you last summer," Asa says. "At 22:02 tonight. Language matches your earlier post calling for removal. Understood."

He turns a page. "Lights," he says. "Rafi."

Rafi lays the router event strip and the Hue log for 00:00 and 00:05. He adds the whitelist entry showing ME-TAB created 04.07 by IP .74, and the cached clients page with the MAC A0:2B:3C:1D:EE:90, vendor Samsung. He adds the floor-cam still from Poetry Night with Margo and the sleeve nick, and the shop speaker's memory screen listing ME-Phone and ME-TAB. He tops it with the tablet photo we shot a half hour ago. Bridge list with Peppermint Cat cached at the top. Routine Test 5min showing Front Bay, 00:00 and 00:05.

"Device label ME-TAB paired to our Hue bridge last week," he says. "Token persisted. At midnight and five past tonight, ME-TAB toggled our light group. Your tablet's routine shows those two toggles and our bridge cached at the top. Your lockbox checks sit at twenty past, forty-three, fifty-eight."

Asa looks at Margo. "Say what you did with the lights."

She holds his eyes for a beat. Her chin tilts. "I ran a test routine," she says. "I wanted the room to reset without drama at the top of a vote."

"You cut the lights," Asa says. "You controlled the room."

She does not answer. Ink records the silence for her.

"Door," he says. "Conrad."

I place the smart lock printout. 00:01:07 unlock by CV-135. Door open. Door closed. Auto-lock. The keypad photo with fresh oil on 1, 3, and 5. The heel smear at the slab and the match to his notch. The refusal card for his call log. And the sentence he dropped in the alley written on a card in my hand.

"Read your line," Asa says.

Conrad looks like a man who would like to negotiate with language and knows he is late. He reads. "She would not sign anything new."

"Thank you," Asa says. "Place yourself."

"I leaned in the dark and pressed her to consider a memo," he says. "I did not touch her."

"Then you stepped to air," Asa says. "At 00:01. Fourteen seconds. Heel matches. Code matches."

Conrad nods once. Pride swallows and sits back down.

"Audio and path," Asa says. "Jenna."

Rafi adds the markers we printed. 23:59:58 ladder squeak. 00:00:03 chair drag and the breath. 00:00:05 lights rise. 00:00:06 thud. He lays the lower shelf board in its sleeve on the table. Two crescent prints nested. Next to it, the bagged tripod head and the bagged inner foot. The spare foot from her tote. The reenactment notes with the tick list and the two photos where her hand reached of its own accord.

"Say it clean," Asa says to her.

She keeps her gaze on the board sleeve. "I reached for my tripod to juice downloads," she says. "I staged a scare at the cut."

"What made the thud," he says.

"The tripod levered the ladder," she says. "It swung. It hit. Panic followed."

"Path," I say. I take the chalk we used earlier and trace the thin gouge we found at the circle. The line aims toward the ballot table, not the exit. I point at the pale blue fiber sealed from the chair back and then at Erica's cardigan draped across its own evidence hanger. I point at the wax scrape color card. Citrus on the left ladder foot. The peel pad we pulled from the blanket seam. The aisle wax bottle. The pad's two fresh crescents. It reads like a recipe. No room for garnish.

"Chair shoved toward the box when the lights cut," I say. "Cardigan fiber on the rail. Tripod foot kissed the lower shelf. Ladder swung into fresh wax. Left foot kept the gray bloom. Right foot lifted. Peel pad later came off on our blanket. The audio fits every step."

Asa looks at the three of them and then at his book. He writes the five closures in a column.

Watermark to Margo.
Timer to Margo.
Door ping to Conrad.
Tripod mark to Jenna.
Wax scrape to aisle.

He turns the notebook to the camera. It sees the words. He sets the book down.

"Now we put it in your mouths on this floor," he says. "In one pass. No spin. You answer to the room you tried to manage."

He points at Margo first. "Your lights."

"I toggled the bulbs with my tablet," she says. "At midnight and five past."

"Your ballots," he says.

"I printed them at ten oh two and brought the stack," she says. "On the old cat's-eye."

"Your goal," he says.

"A vote to remove Erica before she could stall a rent plan," she says. The edges of her words want to fray. She holds them together with force that reads as vanity.

He points at Conrad. "Your door."

"I used my code at twelve oh one and stepped out," he says. "I did not put a hand on the ladder."

"Your aim in the dark," Asa says.

"To force a signature or a promise," Conrad says. "She refused."

He points at Jenna. "Your hands in the cut."

"I reached for my tripod," she says. "I leveraged panic. The rig toppled. I did not intend harm. I staged a scare."

Asa lets the silence walk around the circle once. He looks at each of them and then at the board, the chalk, the gray dust card, the routine shot, the tote sheets. He does not need to raise his voice to make the roof hear him.

"Now the path," he says to me.

I take the chalk and speak while I draw. "Lights dip," I say. "Hands do what they have learned. Margo's thumb loves a toggle. Conrad's jaw loves pressure. Jenna's fingers love a lever. Chair pivots toward the box. The cardigan gives up one pale thread on the back rail. Tripod foot nicks the lower shelf and leaves a crescent. Ladder swings. Left foot skids across our fresh citrus wax and takes on the gray we can smell. Right foot lifts. The thud lands at six when the bulbs begin their climb. The back door wakes at one past. The routine checks itself at five past because people who run rooms like to feel a switch twice."

I set the chalk down. No one speaks.

Havel clears his throat once. He points a pen at the lower shelf sleeve. "We added nothing to that board," he says. "We did not scrub. We did not trace. We photographed, bagged, and carried. It holds the first crescent you put there and the second when we reenacted the reach."

Jenna nods without looking up. She is learning to use a smaller tray of words.

Asa draws a box around his five-line column. He writes a short header. Full scene. He turns the page. His last question comes without windup.

"Margo," he says, "were the lights necessary for safety."

"No," she says. She tries to bite regret onto the last letter and fails.

"Jenna," he says, "was the scare necessary for truth."

"No," she says.

"Conrad," he says, "was the pressure necessary for law."

"No," he says. His voice drops a level. His shoe stops cleaning itself on the rug.

Asa closes his book. He faces the camera and the circle and the ladder sleeve and the cat, who yawns like a judge who never worries about appeals.

"I have what I need," he says.

I breathe. The room breathes. Peppermint hops down, walks the chalk arc with small steps, and sits by the ballot stack. He blinks at Margo once and then turns his head away. Texture, not verdict. The paper gave us the verdict.

Asa lifts the lockbox key from the counter and hands it to me. "Keep the phones," he says. "Release when I call. Next steps go downtown."

"No more blackouts," I say to the circle.

"No more blackouts," he says to me.

Rafi starts to put the cones away, then stops and looks to me. I shake my head. We keep them while the coroner finishes. The aisle earns peace for the rest of the day.

Benji touches the napkin with the croissant and smiles without joy. He will do inventory on Tuesday. He knows where the tapes live. He knows the weight of cardboard at the end of a long morning.

Conrad looks at the back door and then looks away. Progress. He sits straighter. He does not talk.

Jenna wraps both hands around her tote like a person holding a small animal she has named wrong. She will give the name back to the city and it will not be her choice.

Margo smooths her skirt and stares at the stack of ballots in front of her without touching them. Pieces of a plan sit under her fingertips and refuse to obey.

I sweep my eyes across the prints one more time. Volunteer slip. Wrapper sample. Queue. Spool header. Cloud doc. Routine. Router. Whitelist. Speaker memory. Floor cam still. Smart lock log. Keypad photo. Heel match. Audio markers. Tripod foot. Lower shelf board. Ladder foot dust card. Peel pad. Bottle. Wax note. Chair gouge. Fiber. Every page has a neighbor it likes. The case reads like a shelf where nothing sags.

Asa nods at Havel. Havel folds his small map and tucks it into the book where he keeps sentences that win their weight. Rafi caps the camera lens and writes the time on the counter card.

"Time twelve fifty-one," I say for the last image. "Full scene assembled and admitted. Watermark to Margo. Timer to Margo. Door ping to Conrad. Tripod mark to Jenna. Wax scrape tied to the travel aisle. Phones locked. Cones up. Asa says he has what he needs."

Peppermint blinks his slow blink that blesses exactly nothing and still grants calm. I take the key. I take the binder. I take the room back. We will set out cups when the city returns the aisle to us. For now we file the chain and keep the lights where they belong.

CHAPTER 19

Charges Split

The blue wash from the cruisers made the shop's front windows look like aquarium glass. We brought the room outside in one slow, clean line. Cones still at the corners inside. Ladder bagged. Lower shelf boarded and sleeved. Phones locked. Peppermint sat in the window above the display of kid paperbacks and watched the sidewalk as if it were his stage. Texture only. He keeps his own counsel.

The sidewalk on Oak smells like wet concrete and burnt espresso. Sirens off. Radios low. Neighbors held doorways with their shoulders the way this block always does when the night leaves marks. Gran came up from the garage with her ledger hand in her pocket. She gave me a nod that meant I had not embarrassed the family. That nod matters.

Asa set the table on the curb. Not a real table. A crate lid on traffic sawhorses. Clipboard. Case binder. A small evidence mat so property bags do not touch a dirty world. Havel stood at his right like a modest lighthouse. Rafi kept our side, stacking sleeves and receipts, clean as a church pantry.

"Phones stay locked," Asa said. His voice carried without weight. "We will release when booking clears."

The club gathered in a rough ring near the map stand we always roll outside on market days. Benji kept his hands in sight like he had studied the morning and chose calm as a practice. Conrad stood two paces from the back of the ring and kept his eyes off the alley. He needed that practice. Margo squared her shoulders and held still. Jenna leaned on a used utility pole of posture, arms crossed, eyes bright, hungry, afraid of nothing until fear asked for rent.

Two uniforms came from the second car with paper packets already filled. They were not eager. They were not slow. They had faces for this kind of noon.

Asa opened the case binder and set our three spreads where the camera on the cruiser could see them. He did not hold them up. Paper speaks at its own height.

He looked to me. "Call the times," he said.

"Thirteen twelve," I said. "Front sidewalk. Club present. Charges and citations to follow."

He tapped the first packet.

"Jenna Roarke," he said.

She straightened as if someone had said her channel name. For a second she almost put a hand to her hair, then remembered optics and did not.

He read the top line. "Negligent homicide," he said. "For causing the fatal impact through reckless conduct during a planned audio stunt."

She flinched. Small. Real.

"Obstruction," he said. "For concealing the staging intent, misreporting mic placement, and attempting to steer statements away from your rig."

He did not read the rest. He did not need to.

"Turn, please," the taller uniform said.

She turned. Cuffs clicked. Not tight. Not loose. She kept her mouth shut. Good instinct for once. The officer took the tote from her shoulder. I signed the property card for the bagged tripod head and foot and the spare foot from the tote. The officer counter-signed. Chain moved to city hands. Clean.

Jenna looked at me. Not for pity. For framing. I gave her nothing. She tried a line anyway.

"I did not mean harm," she said. It died in the air. Most lines do when the room carries a board that shows your hand on the wrong piece of metal at the wrong second.

The uniform read her rights. She nodded at the right places. When he said counsel, she said yes. When he asked about medicine, she said tea like a joke, then stopped and said no.

As they walked her to the car, her eyes flicked to the lower shelf wrapped in plastic on the sawhorses. The nested crescents looked quiet and final. She shut her mouth and watched her shoes.

Asa tapped the next packet.

"Margo Ellsworth."

She stepped forward a fraction. Pride re-buttoned itself. She left her tote on the curb without being asked. Progress, or theater.

"Tampering," Asa said. "For setting conditions that altered the scene of a vote and a death. Lights. Ballots. Timing."

"False statement," he said. "For denying remote control over our lights while your app listed our bridge and routine. For misrepresenting origin and use of the ballots."

Her chin lifted. "It was a procedural mechanism," she said. Her voice reached for calm and landed on brittle.

"It was your mechanism," he said. "That is the charge."

He nodded at the uniform. No cuffs yet. The officer took her tablet. I signed the property card, listed the device label, the bridge cache screen, the routine screen. Rafi had already printed the screenshots and taped them behind the card. Chain moved. Clean.

"Your counsel," Asa said. "You may call from booking."

She tried to stare him down. Asa has worked longer than most stares. She looked past him at the cat in the window. Peppermint blinked slow and then cleaned his shoulder. He forgives nothing. He keeps time.

Asa tapped the third packet.

"Conrad Vale," he said.

Conrad stepped to the crate lid like a man who knows ceremony can be a sentence. He did not look at the door. He looked at the print that showed his code, the keypad blush, the heel smear.

"Trespass," Asa said. "For using a restricted code during an emergency without a role to do so."

Conrad almost objected and swallowed the sound. He took the citation slip, read the line, nodded. He knows codes and property. He knows what a line like that costs in civil rooms.

"You will also face a tenant complaint," Asa said. "Filed by the moderator's estate to the council through Havel's office. It addresses your attempt to force a signature in bad conditions."

"That complaint will fail," Conrad said, out of reflex. Then he caught himself. "We will see."

"You will," Asa said.

He took the citation again and folded it once, tight. He kept both heels planted. That helped.

I wrote the time on the counter card. "Thirteen nineteen," I said. "Roarke charged. Ellsworth charged. Vale cited. Property receipts signed."

Rafi handed me a strip from the little printer he keeps for events. A summary for the binder and for the porch. I taped it under the window where Peppermint holds court. The tape ran level. He tapped it with a paw and approved. The strip read Closed for police activity. Back soon. People who live here know what that means. People who do not learn faster than they plan.

Gran came to my elbow and looked at the stack of sleeves with her old stamp peeking from a corner. She did not speak. I heard her sentence from the garage anyway. She keeps leftovers. It still landed.

A neighbor from the flower shop across the street brought over a bucket and set it near the curb. Water from her hose glimmered under the squad lights. No one touched it. A kindness is not always for use.

The shorter uniform came back from the car and gave me a small nod. Jenna sat in the back seat with her face set at forward. She had chosen stillness. That will help her later if she learns from it.

Margo stood between two cars with her hands clasped in front of her like a host about to thank donors. She caught me looking and dropped the posture. She glanced at the ballots stacked on the table, the cat's-eye wink on the top sheet, the volunteer slip copy with Gran's blue stamp, and then away. She finally looked tired. Good. Control costs energy. Paper costs more.

Conrad moved to the side and put his back against the brick where the paint fades under the awning. He read his citation a second time and then folded it again. He looked at me.

"You will tell the council I did not touch the ladder," he said. A sentence, not a plea.

"I will tell the truth," I said. "The chair gouge and the wax on the foot do not spell your name. The door at 00:01 does."

He nodded once. He has the sense to take a small win without cheering. He will need that in rooms with wood walls.

Asa gathered the spreads and slid them back into sleeves. He signed the last property card. He took the lockbox key from my hand, opened the lid, and let each person claim a phone under supervision. He kept Jenna's and Margo's locked for booking. He handed Conrad his and wrote the time in the field above his signature on the citation. Conrad said thank you, careful, and stood his ground on the sidewalk.

The ring closed itself. Club members who come for stories and tea stood six feet apart and looked like they had left a church early because the sermon grew teeth. No one recorded. No one clapped. One person held a paper cup halfway to a mouth and forgot to drink.

Rafi stepped to the curb and found me with his eyes. "I will pull the small sign," he said. "No blackouts. No off-network devices. No secret ballots."

"Post it," I said. "Leave it up all week."

He nodded. He likes signs. They call to his sense of order. He went inside to print, hands already doing the job.

Havel moved along the ring like a gentle inspector and touched a shoulder here, a sleeve there, in a way that says the city still has a spine. He stopped at Benji.

"You stay," he said.

Benji dipped his head. "Tuesday," he said.

"Bring a pencil," I said. "You will label the back room ribs until your hand asks for mercy."

He smiled without joy and without complaint. "Good," he said.

A freelancer with a camera came up the block, saw the cruisers, and lifted the lens as if the city owed him a clean shot. Asa turned once and shook his head. It was a small motion. The lens went down. The freelancer backed off and found a crosswalk to lean on.

Asa signed one last line in his book. He did not read it out loud. He does not perform for sidewalks. He handed me his spare pen because he knows I lose mine when the binder gets thick.

"Anything else," he said.

"Keys," I said.

He put his palm out. I laid the ring across it and took it back when he did not close his hand. He smiled with one corner of his mouth, the same look he gives a compliant copier. We both know I would sooner give up coffee than the keys to my lockbox.

"Then we are done," he said. He looked at the ring. "No speeches," he added.

I nodded. "No speeches," I said.

Peppermint stepped down from the window to the register and

then to the stool by the door. He pressed his face against the glass like a bookend and watched the blue lights touch the map stand. He huffed at nothing and then turned his back on the street. He has standards.

The taller uniform guided Margo to the rear car. She climbed in with her tote in the officer's hand and her tablet in a property bag. The door closed. The window stayed up. Her profile held steady. She had a theater face. The show lost an audience. She did not have a line for this.

The shorter uniform slid into the driver's seat of the first car. Jenna stared at the seat head and rolled her shoulders once to ease the cuff. She did not look for the lens. The lens had walked away.

Conrad folded the citation one more time and put it in his inside pocket. He pulled his phone and stared at the black screen without touching it. That restraint looked new on him. I chose to approve.

Gran stepped into the ring and gave Rafi a pat on the arm without softness and then me a look that liked my spine. She tipped her head toward the door.

"Close for an hour," she said. "Then brew something dark."

"Deal," I said.

She looked at the cruiser lights on our windows and at the small sign Rafi had taped to the glass above Peppermint's head. No secret ballots. No blackouts. No off-network devices. She read it once and did not ask to redline. That is respect.

Asa clapped the binder shut. No flourish. He placed it in the canvas bag he uses when he wants to show he is a clerk first. He shook Havel's hand once, then mine, then Rafi's. He kept it light and quick, because this block does not need a show.

"Counsel will call," he said to me. "Send every scan."

"They are ready," I said.

He glanced at the circle. "You run a clean room," he said.

"I like proof," I said.

He walked to the curb and looked both ways like a pedestrian in a city that does not forgive mistakes. He got into the car with the binder on the floor and the radio low. The cruiser eased out from the curb and made the left with a turn signal like a citizen.

The second cruiser followed. The lights stayed on until the block turned from blue to gray again. The front of the shop went back to being glass and wood, not news. People exhaled. Someone coughed. A dog down the block barked twice at a pigeon. The world suggested lunch.

I pulled the door to and turned the small plate on the latch to Closed. I left the sign on the glass. People read it and nodded and walked on. Rafi checked the cones and the tape and the ladder bag and the shelf sleeve because his hands cannot sit still when the room is not yet put away. Benji took the broom out of habit and then looked at me to see if I would stop him. I did not. He set it against the counter and stood in the ring like everyone else.

"Move along," a neighbor said to no one in particular and to everyone enough. It worked.

We did not clap. We did not hug. We did not invent speeches to make grief feel smart. We stood and let the air cool our faces. We let proof sit on a sawhorse and be ugly and plain. We let the street go back to being itself.

Peppermint head-butted the glass where my hip would be if I stood inside. I pointed at him. He blinked. That was our talk.

Rafi came back out with a fresh strip of paper from the little printer. He had written one more line for the day. Club resumes next week with rules posted. He taped it under the first strip and smoothed the corners with his thumb. The paper caught the last bit of blue from a puddle and then dried to the color of rules.

Asa's last sentence sat in my head and found its chair. I did not say it out loud. No one needed it repeated.

The club stood in a quiet ring.

IVY GRANT

No speeches.

CHAPTER 20

Club Reset

Morning brings the kind of light that forgives floors. The travel aisle holds its cones. The bagged ladder rests on the blanket like a sleeping tool. The lower shelf board leans in its sleeve against the counter. Our sign on the glass reads No secret ballots. No blackouts. No off-network devices. Rafi printed it in large type that leaves no gaps for spin.

I unlock, sweep once, and set the counter binder where it belongs. Peppermint inspects each corner like a small inspector with paws. He sniffs the cones, blinks at the ladder bag, and patrols the chalk ghost. Texture. No verdicts.

Gran arrives with her ledger tucked under her arm and a pen that has outlived three city councils. She studies the room. Her eyes track prints, tape, labels. She sets the ledger on the counter and waits.

"Rules," she says.

I pull a sheet of card from the drawer. I write three lines in block letters. No secret ballots. No blackouts. No off-network devices. I date the corner and add the club name. Then I flip the card and print the same lines again so no one can claim they missed it when the wind takes a notion.

Rafi brings a hole punch and a length of twine. He has the pot on already. The shop fills with the smell that rescues mornings and witnesses. He threads the card, ties a clean square knot, and hands me the loop. I hang the sign on the moderator's chair. Not for show. For memory.

Gran signs the back of the card under the date. G. Wren, witness. Her pen clicks back into her pocket with satisfaction. She watches me set a copy on the bulletin board, another on the inside of the front door, and a third in the office window above the file cabinet where it will annoy exactly one person and that person is me. Good. Annoyance keeps habits in line.

Rafi sets mugs by the register. "One for Gran," he says, "one for the clerk, one for the cat." He pours mine and hers. Peppermint gets his saucer of water on the stool. He dips a paw and licks as if he invented sanity.

I check the lockbox. Empty. Key on the ring. I log the chain handoff from Asa's crew at dawn to me. Property lists signed. Phones returned. Tablets in evidence downtown. One line, two initials, done. The binder closes without complaint.

We move through the room with small fixes. Rafi rehabs the chalk outline so it becomes a faint arc only we will notice. He pulls the cones and stores them under the counter. He wipes the map stand and sets a fresh brochure in place of the tote scuff. He tests the Hue bulbs and then deletes every bridge token that is not ours, then logs that deletion. I change the Guest password and tape the new sheet under the counter until we print the small placard for tonight.

Gran goes to the bulletin board and sorts the old flyers. The yard sale with no date goes down. The poetry reading gets a new time now that the city owns last night's hour. She pins the no-ballot rule top center. She does not angle. She goes level. Her thumb leaves a clean crescent on one pushpin head. That is the only crescent I want today.

Customers trickle. Two tourists who read about the cat. One neighbor who pretends to need a gift and needs coffee more.

They read the window strip. They see the cones gone. They look at the ladder bag and then at me. No questions. The city knows when to keep its mouth shut.

I put the lower shelf board on the back counter and tape a note to it for Asa. Ready to release when you say. I set a backup board from our spare stack into the travel shelf bracket. It slides in like a promise. Rafi screws it down. He runs a cloth over the varnish. He breathes in and lets it go. "It will hold," he says. It does.

We reset the circle. Four chairs. Two spares. No tote table. The lockbox sits on a stool with the key under the mat. I print a second small placard and tape it to the box lid. Phones sleep here. No exceptions. I do not hold a vote. I post a rule. Clubs run on posted rules, not whispers.

Peppermint jumps to the moderator's chair and tests the new sign with a head bump. The twine holds. He inspects the knot, approves, and jumps down to perform a slow survey of the rug. He ends at the chair again, then leaves it alone like a cat who understands symbols.

By nine, Gran has a short line at the counter for signatures. She set out the witness form. Members sign to acknowledge the posted rules. No pledge. No drama. A line, a date, a name. Proof a person read a card. Rafi registers memberships renewed last month with a stamp beside each signature. He writes two receipts for the coffee tin, signs, and tucks them into the file. He loves receipts the way cats love heat.

I call Asa. He picks up on the second ring. We swap exact sentences. Ladder bag and shelf board will sit through lunch. He will send the release order this afternoon if the medical examiner clears the head wound timing. He says it clean and then he says nothing else. I thank him for speed. He says it is the work. Calls end. Rafi logs the call on the counter card. Time, duration, purpose. His handwriting is a relief after a night of people who think their hands belong to strangers.

At ten, a woman from the florist brings two stems of eucalyptus.

She slides them into the jar by the map stand and says, "Take the edge off floor smells." I thank her and write a receipt that reads Gift from across the street. She laughs and calls me a menace. Gran smiles at that like a cat that pretends to nap and listens to every word.

I sit at the office desk and write one card for the file. This is the card that belongs to nights like last night, and it will live on top of the stack where anyone who asks for a summary gets detail instead. I print the lines without flourish.

Club Reset, 04.15, morning. Posted rules: No secret ballots. No blackouts. No off-network devices. Witness: G. Wren. Admin: L. Wren. Staff: R. Morales. Phones in lockbox by default. Guest Wi-Fi password updated, bridge tokens purged. Ladder bag and shelf board held pending release. Circle re-set. New lower shelf installed. Signage visible from door, counter, office window.

I flip the card and write the last two lines in thicker strokes because I want them to outlast my mood.

Control invites harm. Proof keeps the room honest.

I sign and tape it to the inside cover of the case binder so the sentence faces whoever opens it next.

Gran appears at my shoulder. She reads the two lines and taps her fingernail on the word proof. "Put it on the website," she says. "And on the invoice footer." She is not joking. I nod and add a sticky note to my keyboard. She watches me write it. She leaves when the note sits where it belongs. Her version of a smile touches one corner of her mouth and goes about its day.

The first club member to arrive is Ruth from the book cart down the street. She's seen every kind of city meeting since film cameras wore leather. She takes a seat, looks at the sign on the moderator's chair, and gives me a nod that doesn't ask for conversation. Second is a college kid who came last month with a thesis on endings. He signs the witness sheet, pockets his phone without needing a prompt, and reads the rules again like they are a poem. Third is the mail carrier, off shift, who sits and sips water and stares at the floor with the gratitude of a person who sorts envelopes for a living and wants to sit where nothing needs sorting for ten minutes.

We do not convene. We just sit until the room remembers how to be a room.

Jenna's chair stays empty. It will stay empty awhile. Margo's list disappears from the board. Conrad's code goes on administrative hold until the council hearing. I write those lines into the club ledger without adjectives. The pen does not hesitate. Paper never flinches.

Rafi brings the pot to the circle table and sets down mugs. He does not ask who wants sugar. People know their own cups. He places the creamer, then moves it an inch so it lines up with the card that reads No blackouts. He pretends he does not care about symmetry. He cares.

Gran stands by the door and becomes witness to the morning in her quiet way. She opens, turns the small plate to Open, and signs the witness log beside the motion. She returns the pen to the cup. She finds the crack in the floorboard by the mat and nudges it with her toe until it sits flush. She steps aside to let two teenagers in with backpacks and a question about mystery paperbacks that do not waste time. "Top shelf, left of the fan," she says. They go where she points without argument.

At eleven, I draft the short post for the club feed. No leading lines. No speeches. Three rules in a list. A time for next week. A note that Erica's family will share memorial details through the council office. I add a line that makes my throat tight and leave it anyway. We will read in her name and count what matters in daylight.

I publish. The post bounces through phones across the block. Responses start with small hearts and then switch to words. I ignore the hearts. I answer the words with schedule and clarity. No call for comments. No debate. That can live on a sidewalk if someone needs it. Not here.

The door bell rings for the first time since the cruisers left last night without setting teeth on edge. It rings like a bell, not a trigger. Two old friends who never agree on Tolstoy come in and ask if the back table is free for an hour. I point. They sit. They read. They disagree with style. The sound is medicine.

I pull the blind on the office window up two inches so the room can see the sun slide along the binder. Peppermint jumps to the sill, steps into the light, and becomes a small statue of himself. He watches the street and then closes his eyes. He naps with one ear turned toward the counter as if he wants to hear when I write the next card. He will.

Late morning brings a delivery from the lab. The envelope holds our ink age report from last week's case. I sign the receipt, scan the report, and slide the original into the related binder under the divider marked First Truth. We keep all our proof even when the news cycle moves on. The practice feels like washing hands. You do it because you respect what comes next.

Asa texts a single line. Release ladder and shelf. I reply Received. I set my phone down face up and write the time on the counter card. Rafi brings the sleeve to the back room, removes the bag, and returns the ladder to its hook with a clean set of pads. He logs the install. He files the bag in a box marked Ended. The lower shelf board stays on the back counter until the family visits, then returns to our storage closet with a tag that says Never sell. Some objects belong to the file forever.

Gran comes back with a small brass bell from a drawer. It once sat on the register when cash drawers stuck. She carries it to the circle and sets it on the table beside the moderator's chair, near the rules card. "If a person needs the room's ear," she says, "they ring once, in the light." No one jokes. Everyone understands what an object can do.

We hold a moment with eyes open. Then we let the bell be a bell.

A kid with a library card asks for a recommendation with a villain who loses the right way. I hand him a paperback that asks for patience and pays it back with a reveal that would make Erica smile. He tucks it under his arm like a secret he intends to keep for two days only. He pays in coins and one clean bill. I print a receipt and write Enjoy the ending on the top. He folds it with care and sticks it in his pocket. He reads the rules on the door as he leaves and gives the sign a thumbs up. I pretend not to see, then smile at the register screen.

Noon arrives without drama. The pot drains. Rafi rinses the cone and sets a fresh one. Gran takes a seat near the back and fixes the program calendar with a sharpened pencil. She boxes the month, adds the blackout ban to each week, and circles the date of Jenna's hearing without crowding the box. She does not label it. She does not have to.

I put one more copy of the rules above the breaker. Rafi adds a physical toggle lock that prevents a cut without a key. He logs the change and tapes the key number to the inside of the breaker door where only staff will see it. He loves this step. I let him enjoy it.

The council clerk stops by with a brown envelope for me to sign. Notice of complaint received. Tenant hearing scheduled. She watches me read, then points to a line. "You will attend?" she says. "To present the timeline for the vote?" I nod and say yes. She thanks me for clean records. She buys a bag of beans and refuses a discount. She adds a dollar to the coffee tin. Tiny acts keep rooms intact.

Late lunch brings the copy shop owner with a squeegee and the exact solvent that removes window ghost rings. He hates dirty glass the way I hate sloppy chain. He cleans the chamber pattern off the bottom blank we had pinned for reference. The board stays sleeved and labeled. The glass gets a second chance. He refuses payment and steals a cookie from the plate near the register. I write a receipt that reads Cookie for glass. He tucks it behind his ear and leaves.

Before closing, I build a small display near the circle that is not a shrine and not a stunt. Five paperbacks Erica argued for. A card that reads Read these out loud to someone you trust. No dates, no flowers, no speeches. Rafi adds a small bowl of paper tabs so people can write a line they loved without names. He tapes a second bowl for tape. He lines it up under the sign. He adds a pencil. He steps back and nods. The table looks like work. Good.

I take the binder from the counter and move it to the office shelf labeled Current. I slide my card with the two lines into the front sleeve. Control invites harm. Proof keeps the room honest. I stand there for a beat, not for drama, for calibration. Then I close the door and go back to the floor.

Members settle into chairs as afternoon shades run across the rug. A few new faces fill the edges. We do not take a roll call. We do not pass a box. We sit. We read a page each from the paperbacks on the small display. We stop when the bell on the table asks us to stop. One ring. Light on. No dip. The room hears the rule and obeys.

When the last page lands, I stand by the moderator's chair. I do not sit in it. I hold the back rail with my left hand and look at what this morning fixed. Rules posted. Tokens purged. Bridge locked. Door codes revised. Witness log signed. Salts and sugars where adults can see them. Nothing behind flaps or under sleeves. The simple things run the day.

"Next week," I say. "We bring a short list of books with endings that earn themselves. We read in Erica's name. We accept disagreement in full light. We hold no secret paper. If you want to vote on snacks, we raise hands. The cat does not count."

Soft laughs make it to the ceiling and stop there. Good. The room found its shape again.

We close at six. Gran signs the witness log one more time. She writes Good day next to her name. She leaves the pen in the cup, tap-taps the mat crack with her shoe, and goes home with her ledger like a dignitary.

Rafi does the last sweep. He checks the breaker lock, the router admin, the bridge whitelist, the Guest password card, the lockbox key. He points at each one. I nod. He washes the pot and sets it to dry upside down like a small bell. He leaves it so the drip lines look like art. He kills the dimmer and leaves the front bay on a soft level that tells the street we are closed and not hiding.

Peppermint climbs the moderator's chair. He circles once to test the sign rope. It holds. He kneads the seat cushion with bread-making focus, then drops to his side and goes to sleep with his chin on the rail. He snores in little puffs. His tail thumps once, twice, then goes still.

I take one last photo for the binder. Sign on chair, bell on table, ladder on hook, shelf set, cones gone, cat asleep. Today's paper sits on the counter corner. I write the time on the counter card. Then I write one line in the binder under my two-line card.

Room reset, proof posted, peace restored.

I turn the small plate on the door to Closed, lock up, and leave the lights on a warm level that keeps nothing secret and nothing harsh. On the way out I touch the sign on the moderator's chair. It swings a thumb of space and falls back.

Control invites harm.

Proof keeps the room honest.

END OF BOOK FOUR

PEPPERMINT CAT BOOKSHOP MYSTERIES

ABOUT THE AUTHOR

IVY GRANT

Ivy Grant is a celebrated fiction author best known for her gripping mysteries and heart-racing adventure novels that blend sharp intellect with atmospheric storytelling. Born in a quiet coastal town where fog rolled in like secrets, Ivy grew up with a fascination for hidden things—locked drawers, whispered rumors, and maps that didn't quite match the terrain.

Ivy remains famously private, rarely giving interviews and preferring to let her characters do the talking. When she's not writing, she's said to be hiking through storm-lashed moors, sketching story ideas on café napkins, or cataloging antique keys she insists will someday open something extraordinary.

THANK YOU.

Printed in Dunstable, United Kingdom